Whispers from Beyond

30 Miniature Tales

A. R. Redington

Dovian's Journal: Gold Status Publishing

Dovian's Journal: Gold Status Publishing

www.ARRedington.com

ISBN: 978-1-958038-04-8

BOOKS BY A. R. REDINGTON

The Esoteric Design

The Esoteric Design: Disbanding Hope

The Esoteric Design: Civilization Lost

Predator: Eyes of the Demon, The Trophy

Masters of the Ellem

The Trouble with Mystery

Whispers from Beyond: 30 Miniature Tales

DEDICATION

To those who struggle with writer's block or any form of creative block.

You are not alone.

CONTENTS

AUTHOR'S NOTE

This book started as a project to help with writer's block. The criteria involved 30 days of writing, using a new theme each day based on a single keyword or phrase. The majority of the word list was from a prompt I found online. You can find many of these online or generate your own random word lists; there are no strict rules. I started the assignment in October, which led to many horror/thriller-based themes. Though most of the book fits the horror genre, there are touches of fantasy and sci-fi throughout. The point of this assignment was to write whatever was inspired by the daily word, regardless of genre. Therefore, this book contains different themes, plots, and styles. Honestly, I enjoy some stories; others I wouldn't claim to be my best work, but this is also an example to those who struggle to write or finish a project.

Realistically, I would have stuck with the plan every day for 30 days. However, I still struggled with what seemed like such a minimal task. Rather than feel guilty, I set the project aside as life continued its many twists and turns. Because of this, some stories are a couple of years old, and some are brand new, as I recently finished the project. Also, a few of these are excerpts for larger projects that I wish to publish in the future. Another is an easter egg to a previously published series. Whether or not you are having a good creative day, the point is to eventually write and finish your projects, even if it takes much longer than anticipated. The goal isn't to be perfect or timely. The aim is to finish, no matter what, no matter how long it takes.

PUMPKIN

LITTLE VICTORIA sat upon the wrought iron fence, kicking her feet back and forth as she stared at the pale moon of the midnight sky. It was larger than usual, and she wondered if that meant it was closer, brighter, or had merely grown in size like her tummy used to when she overindulged in Mr. and Mrs. Kaplan's baked pies. A dense fog eddied low across the dirt roadway in front of her, a chill wind carrying dead leaves along with it.

The clip-clop of hooves echoed in the distance, attracting her attention. She narrowed her eyes. Rarely a man journeyed along this path, especially at this time of night. An oversized silhouette formed within the mist, tall and dark—a man on a giant horse. An excited whinny blared into the night, and Victoria smiled.

"It is Mr. Irving and Sir Washington!" she happily declared.

The horse and man neared her position; the clopping hooves provided a parading fanfare as they approached the iron gate. The young girl smiled and waved. Mr. Irving's shoulders turned toward her as Sir Washington reared, crying out. She wasn't sure what the actual names of the man and his horse were. Mr. Irving never spoke, but she felt it odd not to have a proper title, so she made up her own, which she believed to be very fitting. The man never protested, and so the labels remained.

"It's been countless nights since you paid me a visit, Mr. Irving!" Victoria hopped off the fence and strolled toward the man and his horse. "How is Sir Washington? He seems a bit bonier than last I saw him."

Mr. Irving remained silent as the girl inspected the horse's hooves. Black goo covered the front right foot, where a chunk of flesh had fallen off the leg, revealing dried and torn muscle and a bit of bone. The girl patted the horse's neck with a frown, inspecting Sir Washington's blood-red eye and muzzle, which looked about as poorly as his legs. On one side, a pair of ribs shimmered white in the moonlight.

"He needs to eat," Victoria scolded Mr. Irving, who sat straight as a board upon his saddle, his leather-covered hands tightly gripping the reins. "And I dare say you don't look much better. Where has your head gone? Did you lose it once again?"

Irving's shoulders slumped, a gesture that told her he was slightly disappointed and perhaps a little tired. She couldn't remember ever seeing the man's actual head. Still, frequently, he wore a replacement, usually something Victoria had made up herself—makeshift visages of clay, cloth, and even autumnal vegetables.

"No matter! I have just the thing!" The girl skipped away, capturing a plump orange pumpkin beside the entrance gate. "I was bored earlier, so I carved this! I think it is quite lively, don't you?"

Mr. Irving turned a bit toward her, still offering no words, as would be difficult for a man without a head. The pumpkin was enormous in her hands but appeared to be about the right fit for his shoulders. A pair of carved eyes and a crooked smirk decorated its surface. Leaning forward, a large hand reached toward the girl. She happily dropped the gourd into the man's palm. Without much more than an invisible glance, Mr. Irving placed the pumpkin directly where his head should be. After some twisting and adjusting, he peered down at Victoria with a sizeable black smile.

"I think it lacks something," she said, holding her chin.

Mr. Irving nodded and snapped his fingers; a yellow blaze sputtered to life inside, illuminating his features. Victoria giggled and clapped.

"Perfect! That is much better! I must say, I think this is my favorite look for you. Any time you lose your head, be sure to come back to me, and I shall make you another." Victoria twirled, eyeing the pumpkin patch that lay on the horizon in a faraway field. "I shall take stock to hold us over for the rest of the season…just in case."

Mr. Irving remained silent, but he did manage a short nod. After a moment, he returned his attention to the small town occupying the forest's edge. It mostly lay dark save for the glowing lanterns lining the main road and a few windows. Smoke seeped from the chimneys, the scent carrying on the breeze. Victoria followed his gaze, eyeing the sleepy little town.

"You're going into town, aren't you?" she asked. There was no response. "Well…as you most likely are, it may be pertinent to know that little Billy Kaplan passed away the other day."

Mr. Irving met her stare, and Victoria continued. "Turns out, he drowned unexpectedly in the river on the edge of town. But whispers on the wind say it was no accident. Mrs. Kaplan had become quite friendly with Mr. Parker in recent years. A few quiet rumors spread that Billy wasn't Mr. Kaplan's child but Mr. Parker's instead. It seems the allegations reached Mr. Kaplan's ears, and not long after, he and Billy went on a fishing trip, where the boy met his untimely end. Tripped and hit his head on a rock, says Mr. Kaplan."

Irving looked toward the town, his fiery eyes narrowing.

"But I know the truth," Victoria sang. "For I spoke with Billy before he crossed over. Mr. Kaplan knocked him upside the skull with a rock and then held the poor boy underwater for a whole ten minutes!"

Squeezing the reins, Mr. Irving prepared to ride forward. Sir Washington snorted, the animal's red eyes looking straight ahead.

"You know, it's been an awfully long time since I had one of Kaplan's delicious pies. Despite being a mean, crotchety man, Mr. Kaplan surely knows how to bake." Victoria lightly kicked at a small rock. "I think it would be nice to share a warm apple pie with you before you disappear again."

Mr. Irving pulled back on the leather straps, and Sir Washington reared, neighing like a wild beast. Without another word, the pumpkin-headed specter and his horse sped off into the foggy night toward the small town. Victoria turned to look toward the cemetery behind her, passing through the gate entry. She'd sit atop her stone, gleefully awaiting the return of her friend, for she knew that despite his scary exterior, he would be kind and thoughtful enough to bring her some pie.

She played with a trinket lying across her tombstone. It had been many years since her own family, close and extended, laid flowers on her grave. However, Mr. Irving always returned with a gift in thanks for any information regarding the latest victim of the atrocities that occurred within the small, dark town. It was home to an extensive list of filthy crimes and corruption, governed by a society that protected its own. After Victoria's murder, she made it her pastime to avenge those who similarly met their end. And for those who appeared within the cemetery—lost and confused—she helped guide them to the other side. The girl could leave whenever she wanted but chose to stay in the cemetery until she felt she had assisted enough, and the ugly, dark secrets would come to an end. Besides, it wasn't entirely lonely. She had Mr. Irving and Sir Washington.

A scream roared in the distance, and one by one, the windows of the small town lit up, a few more shrieks following in panic throughout the streets as the frightening specter took his revenge upon Mr. Kaplan. Victoria smiled.

She could nearly smell the pastry from where she sat, and then she wondered if he would also bring her a slice of pumpkin pie.

CABLES

CHARLES WORKED in IT for the majority of his life. At fifty years old, everyone thought he would have grown tired of the same old thing. However, Charles had OCD. He couldn't help but do the same things each day. On top of that, everything had to be tidy. He had been born with an obsessive condition, but it worsened with age. As long as Charles had his IT career, he'd remain happy despite the pay cuts, poor benefits, and abusive colleagues.

At 5 am each morning, Charles awoke by his third alarm. He sat up, stretched, yawned loudly, and popped his back as always. By 5:30 am, the man had finished his shower and fed his cats named Abigail, Betty, and Cindy. He loved animals as long as they were female and preferred to stay away from the males; the same went for humans. Women were kinder to him than men were. His male peers bullied him his entire life, and more often than not, it was a woman who came to his rescue or helped bandage his cuts and bruises.

By 6:00 am, Charles ate his breakfast of slightly burnt toast and eggs with a small glass of orange juice and a large thermos of coffee, which he would refill before heading to work. He took the bus because they ran on better schedules than anything else in the city. He never liked driving anyway. Other motorists were too unpredictable, as was the weather. He arrived at his final stop by 6:45 daily and reached his office by 6:50 am. Never once had he clocked in past 7:00 am.

"Oh, hey, Charles! How's it going?" Raymond asked. He adjusted his blue tie against his white collar. With his slicked hair and golden wristwatch worth half of Charles' salary, Raymond reflected the expected style of such a prestigious organization that handled billions of dollars for some of the world's largest corporations and wealthiest elites. The company treated Raymond and the others like kings compared to Charles, the lowly IT man.

Charles walked past his coworker without much more than a quick "morning."

"Listen, Charles; there was an incident last night." The man sat at his desk and spun his scissors around one finger, a habit that always made Charles nervous.

"What, what did you do now?" Charles asked, pushing his glasses further up his nose. "Every day I come in, there's something screwed up."

Raymond laughed and shrugged. "Hey, it's not me! It's those gremlins."

Charles scoffed and walked away, his mind churning over which possible disaster he'd have to deal with that day. "Gremlins. Stupid gremlins," the man grumbled. "Not even real! Gremlins aren't real!"

"The whole system is down! We can't do anything until it's up again," Raymond shouted as he sipped his coffee, watching the older man stroll around the corner.

Charles' coworkers were incompetent. They couldn't handle spreadsheets, the internet going down for maintenance, sending simple emails, following the rules of using no social media while on the clock, or using the printer. At first, the more troublesome issues seemed harmless enough—glitches in the software and errors in the code. Charles would leave work with the system running perfectly only to have it be a royal mess the next day, further convincing him that someone was sabotaging his work after hours, which no one was ever allowed to go into his office. After many months of toying with the code and upgrading everything he could think of, things quieted down. That is, until a week ago when the hardware throughout the facility started breaking and frying for no reason.

With his many complaints, nothing ever got done about the damages. Nobody was caught, reprimanded, or fired for the destruction of property. Charles was left alone in his basement office beneath everyone else to solve the persistent problem. However, since the issues always occurred after he left the office, it was logical to assume the damages were made in malice. Because of this, Charles set up a few security cameras throughout the basement to overlook his workstation, the mainframe, and the countless wires he so meticulously organized daily—a wall of neatly coiled and lined color-coded cables.

"It's harassment! Simple as that!" Charles stomped down the cement stairs to the lower level of the facility. "Raymond and his buddies have had enough laughs at my expense! I'll catch them red-handed one of these days, and then they'll be sorry."

Unfortunately, the security cameras had proven to be useless. The devices encountered a glitch each night, shutting off for about fifteen minutes, never catching the culprit who caused so much trouble.

Charles rounded the corner and jumped back as an electric spark snapped in his direction. He gaped in horror at his wall of wires. The cables hung limply—cut, torn, and mangled—trailing across the floor in bits and pieces. The mess was beyond some terrible prank; it was downright outrageous and blatant destruction of property. Someone was after his sanity, and he had a good idea of who it was.

The memory of Raymond's smug grin as he spun his scissors made Charles' blood boil. Infuriated, he rushed to the main level, where Raymond worked alongside his cronies. Of course, the man wasn't at his desk. Charles headed for the breakroom, where many of the employees wasted the majority of their day drinking espresso and sneaking cigarettes.

"It's one hell of a mess down there," Raymond's voice rang out. Charles halted outside the door, listening in on the gossip.

"I heard it's all been ripped to shit," another man said.

"It's completely useless; we'll have nothing to do all day until Charles fixes it. Not sure if he can," Raymond continued.

"Hey! Nothing wrong with that, am I right?"

A flurry of laughter filled the room.

"Charles will lose his job soon if he can't get all this straightened out."

"Once again, nothing wrong with that, right?"

Another swill of laughter echoed down the hall. Charles' hands balled into fists. He knew it. They were trying to get him fired.

"In all seriousness, though, I'm going down there tonight," Raymond replied.

"I knew it!" Charles barked as he entered the room. "Mutiny! Conspiracy! Do you have any idea of what you've done?"

"What the hell are you droning on about now?" Raymond asked.

"Man's crazy. What conspiracy?" One of the others chimed in.

Charles cowered beneath the group's stare, trembling at the memories of when bullies had nearly beaten him within an inch of his life in high school due to his strange behavior and "dorky" clothing.

"I, I…I will not be leaving this p-place! It's my job; it's my life! I'll prove it. I know you're the one who has been m-messing up everything!" Charles stammered.

"Easy, old man. Nobody's touching your stuff. As if we have half the brains even to mess it up anyway," Raymond deflected.

"Anybody can mess with the coding. And any dolt can destroy hardware and delete files off the network! The cables are ruined! This will take more than a day to fix." Charles huffed, preparing for the possibility of a fight.

Raymond and the others gaped at each other. Nobody else said anything, and the leader of the group sighed. "Accuse all you want, but we have nothing to do with it. In fact, I'm just as annoyed by it as you are. We have clients to take care of, and we can't do that if things aren't working properly."

"We can't do much either while you're up here yelling at us like a lunatic," another man said.

Laughter followed once again. Charles hung his head in defeat and backed away. Raymond, however, didn't look amused. His eyes were cold and calculating. It was a look that Charles had attributed most predators to have. Not wanting further harassment, the timid man wandered back to the safety of his refuge in the basement, where he would spend the remainder of the day ordering new cables and repairing what he could with his limited tools. However, Charles wasn't about to give up the battle. He would wait until after hours to catch the culprit red-handed.

Right at 5 o'clock, he clocked out as usual. A creature of habit, it went against his nature not to return home by the first bus, make tea, and catch the evening news. Instead, he waited by the street corner until the occupants departed and the lights to the interior dimmed. A few moments later, two of the men from the breakroom who often followed Raymond's footsteps rushed out of the building.

"I told you that place was haunted! I'm not going back!" one man shouted as they hurried along the sidewalk away from Charles.

Raymond never exited the building.

"I knew it," Charles whispered, heading for the entrance. Peeking inside, he noticed Raymond wasn't at his desk. The man's heart raced with fear and excitement as he neared the staircase to the basement. Readying to catch Raymond in the act of destruction, Charles lifted his cell phone, recording his travel down the steps.

He heard a strange noise followed by a shout, then an electrical crackle. Frightened, he waited around the corner, listening as a series of snaps and pops echoed within the cold, dank room, followed by a strange chittering sound. Charles used his phone's camera to look around the corner. He licked his lips with anticipation as he prepared to shout his 'ah-ha.' Instead, Charles froze at what his camera revealed to him.

Lying on the floor, tied up by the cables, sat Raymond. A bloody gash lined his forehead and cheek, and red saturated the collar of his overpriced dress shirt. If it wasn't Raymond destroying everything, then who was it?

A strange tittering clicked in Charles' ear as his cellphone's battery suddenly drained, and its screen faded, but not before capturing a split-second glimpse of a small grouping of strange critters passing across the end of the hall in front of Raymond.

Charles screamed, tumbling away from the strange being that latched onto the wall beside his head. It was roughly the size of a cat and looked slightly like a round monkey with sharp teeth but had thick, bushy hair and orange eyes with barely a pupil. In response to Charles' outburst, it hissed and sprung onto the floor beside his feet.

"What, what are you?" Charles asked.

Raymond groaned from the opposite side of the room, the cables crackling around him. Four more of the little beasts surrounded the white-collared man, licking their lips. They took turns shocking him while taking swigs of the electric current snapping from the severed ends of the cords.

"Are, are you going to eat him?" Charles asked. They all paused, and each of the orange eyes peered at him. "Are you going to…eat…eat me?"

The creature beside Charles' foot slowly moved closer, eyeing him curiously.

"My God, you really are gremlins, aren't you? You're the ones destroying my work. You've been eating my cables like spaghetti."

The creature bounced with recognition and laughed, a buzzing, chortling noise. The others at the end giggled as well and danced, poking Raymond with the popping wires.

"Listen, uh…can we make a deal?" Charles whispered.

The one closest to him cocked its head to the side, listening.

"If I…uh…let you eat him, will you leave my work alone? I don't want to lose my job, and I enjoy working in the basement. Though it does get lonely, I usually don't like others in my workspace. However, I'd be willing to allow you to remain here, and maybe I can find some old gadgets or batteries for you to chew on. In exchange, you can have…him." Charles peered at Raymond, who groaned, his eyes rolling in his skull as he lifted his head.

"What are you doing, Charles?" he asked with a slurring murmur.

The fuzzy critters chittered to one another, jumping and snickering like children. The one closest to Charles tapped his shoe, gave a peculiar little nod, and then affirmed to the others their new orders. Charles' heartbeat slowed as relief overtook him. The gremlins seemed wise and interested in upholding their end of the deal.

"I'm taking care of the problem, Raymond," the older man spoke as he adjusted his glasses.

The gremlins crawled toward the tied-up man. Raymond squirmed, pressing further against the wall.

"Charles! Are you insane!? Help me!" Raymond screamed.

"I, I can't do that. They are hungry, and I have to uphold my end of the bargain. You know how it is. It's a dog-eat-dog world."

Charles watched with keen interest as the gremlins pounced upon his coworker, biting and clawing him while using the cords to electrocute and cook him. The sight didn't bother Charles as much as the smell did. He would certainly need to invest in an air purifier and some incense. And when they had finished, the critters were thoughtful enough to help with the mopping. Though the definition of their help resulted in spilled water, Charles overlooked it as it seemed, for the first time in his life, outside of his cats, he may have made some friends. Charles spun with the mop in hand, singing and laughing while the gremlins circled him, twirling and chanting in their guttural way.

Raymond was the first. If the creatures would become restless and start causing trouble again, Charles would simply have to lure another food source into the basement. And with how his coworkers treated him, he already had a long list of names lined up.

TIME

TIME. IT'S a thing often taken for granted. Every manager and business owner carefully scrutinizes each minute in today's world as they try to drain every ounce of lifeforce from their employees for each penny spent. Humankind measures the seconds occupied by such careers that make them wish they would die in their sleep before the alarm sounded to send them off to the dreadful workforce each day. For many, life has become a spectacle of counting down the minutes until one can go home, watch television, and go to bed to repeat the cycle again and again.

Where has the time gone? Is it New Year already? My, look how much he has grown; I remember when he was only yea high!

David was one such man who lived his day-to-day life counting down the minutes and sometimes seconds before he could clock out and go home. Still, he wasted every precious moment watching repeats of his favorite shows. David didn't hang out with his friends as often as they wanted him to. He rarely called his mother, who had passed away far too soon, in his eyes. And his dad, well, he rested in a nursing home in nearly a vegetative state. David spent his nights on the couch with a pack of beer and nothing else. He didn't figure he'd ever change, that life would ever amount to anything more than his typical routine. However, his reality transformed when he met a woman named Charlene.

Charlene burst into his life unannounced while eating at the local diner one evening. She was a splash of vibrant color against the dull landscape of his life. Charlene was loud, energetic, and happy, unlike anyone David had ever known. After spending one evening with her, he knew he had to have her as his own. Rumors around town spread to his ears about a historical superstition involving a Crossroads demon. One deal, that's all he wanted. Charlene was worth the potential curse he would inherit from making such a foolish wager. Whenever she was around, time slowed. She opened his eyes to a world he had never experienced, and he would give anything to spend every minute of his life with her, even if it cost him his soul.

David sat in the car, twiddling his thumbs, his leg bobbing up and down, his attention on the dashboard clock. It was nearly midnight. In only a few more minutes, he would meet his demise. His time with Charlene had come to a close, and tonight would be the night the demon would come to collect. As soon as he had made his wish, David realized his grave mistake. He was cursed. Anything and everything that should have gone right with Charlene had gone wrong. Yet, he could not get rid of her. It started small—habits she developed that made him cringe, her laugh growing more annoying each day, the way she talked with her mouth full. He managed to live with the minor idiosyncrasies, but everything plummeted into a sea of catastrophe after the wedding. She wasn't the woman he had met. Charlene was better than this. Charlene made him feel about himself initially, but then she turned into something far worse than he could have imagined as time went on.

First, she started to gain weight. Her lithe body ballooned up larger than anything David would ever deem attractive. Yet, despite how little they had made love and all the protection they used, she became pregnant three times. The children, things he had never wanted, were loud and dirty. They were all chubby and smelt odd. They were disgusting, noisy, and had all of their mother's unpleasant habits. Soon, the only words that came out of Charlene's mouth were negative. She was unhappy. She hated her life. She doted on him constantly, begged for his attention, and pleaded with David to start over in a new place. Instead, David worked longer hours. He dreaded going home, and any time he was, he counted the minutes until he could leave the house to get some peace in his tiny cubicle.

David hated his life. He disliked his children and loathed his wife. Eventually, the man counted down the days until his contract had run out. For the past year, he had never been more excited to meet his death, to escape the hell known as his life.

"Still counting the minutes? After everything you've received?" an old familiar voice called out. David hopped into his seat, slamming his head into the car roof.

"Received? You cursed me! You ruined everything!" David shouted.

He glared out the windshield at the vaporous form standing before his car. He could barely see the woods behind the demon, the moonlight halfway hidden behind clouds.

"I only did as you asked, David," the demon replied.

"Yeah, and you twisted it all into something horrendous."

The form watched him momentarily before continuing, "I've done no such thing. Anything and everything was kept in its original state. What you have experienced is precisely what you would have experienced regardless of whether my hand was at play. I simply *pushed* the suggestion further into her mind to join you. You are the one who tainted your wish."

David remained silent; his lips pursed tight.

"With every minute you've counted, you have taken your life for granted. Your beautiful wife and children, your house in the suburbs. Your mother and father. You were so preoccupied with the greener side that you never learned to appreciate what you had."

"Beautiful wife?" David scoffed. "That fat cow?"

"The one that you ruined."

"Ruined? How? I didn't force her to eat herself nearly to death."

"No, but her depression played a big part in that, as did working day and night to provide a loving home for you and your children. She homeschooled, fed, clothed, and cleaned up after them. And she did the same for you. And any time you could have come home to spend time with them, what did you do?"

David remained quiet, a tinge of guilt settling in his gut.

"You complained about everything she did. You complained about dinner. You only wanted to watch the same television shows you had seen repeatedly. And, when she needed you the most, you blew her off to spend time with your friends or work overtime. How often did you stay the night at your office to avoid her? Did you even know that she was sick?"

David glanced at the clock. One minute remained. Time had significantly slowed, and it only made him feel nauseous.

"Hurry it up already!" David cried.

"We still have some time, David. I will ensure these final moments are the longest of your life."

The man gnashed his teeth. He had no idea how he was going to meet his death. Would it be a heart attack? Would the demon consume him, or would something more sinister devour him? Or would he be blown to smithereens like in the movies?

"Always thinking of yourself," the demon said in a judgmental tone.

David had driven to the woods to make his death seem accidental or perhaps appear to be a victim of murder. The last thing he wanted was to die in that house with his wife and kids. A pang of regret set in. He barely thought of the effect his death would have on his family. Sure, he hated his life, but they truly didn't deserve the despair they were about to face. How would Charlene pay the bills? His life insurance policy wasn't the greatest. His thoughts conflicted. Why should he care what happened to them? Once he was dead, he was gone. None of it would matter to him anymore. Yet, the thought of Charlene and the kids all alone, having to go through his things and sell the house, left him feeling guiltier than he thought he'd be. At the very least, he could have prepared a will or handled some things beforehand.

He met the demon's dimly lit gaze. "Give me one more day. I…I can change things. Fix them for the better."

"Time's nearly up."

"Just let me say goodbye! Charlene at least deserves that!" David turned on the car and sped into reverse, driving back through the wooded trail until he met the paved street, where he whipped the car around.

He pressed his foot to the floor, speeding back into town. It was nearly an hour's drive, but he had to try. His eyes locked onto the clock of the car. It was now midnight. How would he die? How soon? Would it be a car wreck? He peered through the rearview mirror, trying to catch a glimpse of the demon, a monster, a car, anything. Instead, he only saw the road swallowed by darkness and the slight glimmer of the moonlight. As another minute passed, he allowed a laugh to escape. Perhaps the demon decided to give him a second chance. Still, he wasn't going to risk it, and he continued into his neighborhood, going well over the speed limit. He crashed into the driveway, knocking over the mailbox. Leaving the keys in the ignition, he darted for the house.

"Charlene!" He called out.

The windows of the living room remained lit. It was strange as Charlene always went to bed before him and never stayed up past ten. Slamming against the front door, he nearly fell on his face as he plowed through the entry. Steadying himself, he called out her name again and abruptly fell silent. Charlene stood in the dining room, facing the front door. Her eyes were red, and her face puffy. She had been crying. Her typical ugly bathrobe covered her round body, and she had worn the same old slippers since the day they had married.

"Charlene," David whispered. "Are…are you okay?"

"Okay?" Charlene laughed. Her eyes were wild, nearly aflame as the lamplight reflected in her irises. "Do I look okay to you?"

David stayed in his place, feeling incredibly uncomfortable. Perhaps he shouldn't have let his guilt get the better of him.

"So, who is she?" Charlene asked.

Feeling as if he had been hit by a brick, David shook his head. "Uh, what?"

"Don't play stupid with me! I'm sick of your lies and games! Where were you tonight? Whom have you been seeing?"

David laughed. "Charlene? You…you think I'm cheating on you?"

"I know it! I've called your boss. I yelled at him for making you work so much overtime."

David's face fell.

"And you know what he told me? He said he hasn't been making you work overtime. He said you've been on normal hours. So, quit with your lies!"

"Now, now, I can explain! It's not what you think." David held up his hands as the woman stomped toward him with a look of outrage.

"I have worked so hard to keep this family together! I've done nothing but love you with all of my heart, and you've abandoned us! Our children." Tears streamed down her face. "Me. Us. You gave up on us before it even began."

The man frowned, lowering his head. She was right. He took her for granted just as he did everything else. Pity swirled in his heart. For once, not for himself, but for someone else.

"Well, no more! I'm not dealing with this anymore!" Charlene screamed.

She moved forward, and David opened his arms, preparing to hug and comfort her. He needed to apologize and make things better. As she entered his embrace, he felt a sharp pain in his abdomen, followed by a searing heat as he felt ill, trembling.

"No more!" She screamed, removing the knife from his stomach before plunging it deep inside once again. "Never again!"

David gaped down at himself, watching the silvery blade repeatedly enter his body. One, two, three, four, five. He lost count as the stabbing continued relentlessly throughout his torso. He looked at the grandfather clock, watching the final minute before midnight. Eventually, he no longer felt anything as his wife continued to slice into him. His attention lingered on the clock as it gonged slowly. One, two, three, four, five. It continued up to twelve gongs. And then, he realized another tiny detail about his day. He had already counted the minutes to midnight. He should have died an hour ago. However, this clock was an hour behind to account for daylight savings. Somewhere, he heard the low laughter of the demon.

He lived his final hours twice. Given a false hope due to an extra hour, something he had always taken for granted, he smirked in his last moments, finding it funny to be fooled by time.

HORSE

CRICKETS CHIRPED a melody in the pale moonlight. A fluttering hum sounded in my ear as a moth drifted toward the white light of my painted lamp. It bobbed back and forth, then smacked my forehead before clinking against the glass. I lowered the wick, dimming the light within. One fluttering pest was troublesome enough; I didn't need an entire fleet. It followed my paintbrush, finding the water and turpentine mixture in the mug beside me. As I dipped to clean the bristles, the blasted thing fell into the cup, and its wings instantly melted within the mixture. It couldn't be helped. It wasn't my fault stupid creatures insisted on having their curiosity get them killed. With a flick, I tossed the tiny body into the grass.

By this time, the full moon had pushed itself away from the clouds of the nearing storm. The moonlight, along with my lamp, illuminated the canvas before me. Landscapes were often painted in daylight, portraying the parks and beaches flourishing with villagers and sometimes the attendance of the King and Queen. I preferred images of twilight. Darkness had its beauty. Many didn't understand, claiming I didn't know how to paint in a full range of colors as the other artists. Idiots, they were. My palette may seem limited to them, but it took just as much skill to paint an image with a variety of similar hues that depicted the beauty of the night as it did to paint one with a rainbow display. The contrast of the moonlight edges along the slapping waves, the outlines of the jostling leaves of the trees and grass, the slick shine of the wet rocks, everything had its unique details, one that required touches more than a color differentiation. No, moonlight paintings were just as challenging, if not more, than those made during daylight.

Turn their noses up no matter how much; my skill was proven plenty of times by those who commissioned me. I worked full-time, mainly for those often indisposed by sickness or mental disabilities. They seemed to enjoy the darkness of my work—the visceral details of the lands depicted during a time that many were too afraid to see with their own eyes.

A quiet snort alerted me of a man riding on horseback along the beach. I lowered my brush, keeping an intense gaze. To be out at this hour on this shore was often considered suicide by those of any sound mind. Lucky for me, I was an artist and thus never of sound mind. I continued painting, maintaining sight of the man and his steed. A sword lay strapped to his hip. No armor protected his body, and his head remained uncovered. Judging by his clothing style and the silhouette of his messy hair, I could safely assume he was nothing more than a farm boy. Any closer to the water, and he'd undoubtedly have a problem on his hands.

Just as the thought formed in my mind, the man's horse reared, screeching in a way that nearly sounded like a pig during slaughter—it was frightened. The man shouted for the horse to calm down, but the giant beast did no such thing. Instead, it knocked the rider to the ground and galloped up the hill, as high and far away from the water as it could, toward my position. The man called and chased after it. As he neared me, his unsteady breaths calmed.

"A bit dumb to be in these parts this late," I said.

The man scoffed. "Did you see—?"

"Your horse?" I interrupted. "Yes, over yonder. There's a recently harvested grain field; he'll be safe up there."

"Safe?" the man sighed.

"He's smart. Not much I can say about you, though."

"Excuse me?" The man glared at me with eyes that remained an undecipherable color. Pity. The eyes were my favorite part of a person's portrait, a gateway to their soul, mannerisms, and personality.

"Are you aware of where you are?" I asked, looking around him to add a touch of cool-white paint to the canvas.

"I am."

"And may I ask why you would dare to travel through this area at night?"

"What's it to you? You mind your own business, and I'll mind mine."

I shrugged, "Fair enough." I dabbed my brush onto the palette, mixing another color. "I like to get the back story of those who pass through here. You know, in case they meet their demise soon after."

The man scowled. He didn't feel threatened, but I wasn't trying to be threatening as much as truthful. "I don't believe in that shit. Now, if you don't mind, I bid you goodnight. Besides, aren't you a bit of a hypocrite? Being here at night as well?"

"I'm an artist," I replied. What more could be said?

The man shook his head and began to walk toward the field behind me. Just as he did, a loud whinny echoed through the humid air. I smiled; it was here.

"What was that? It surely wasn't my horse." The man walked ahead of me, eyeing the coastline.

A horse cried from the ocean waters, waves slapping up and over its form.

"My God! How had we not noticed it before?" he shouted.

"Careful," I spoke up as the man motioned to move down the hill. "It may not be what you think it is."

"I don't have time for your superstitious bunk. It is clearly a horse in need of rescuing." He rushed down the hill.

I sighed, dipping my brush into my paints. "Suit yourself."

The horse repeatedly cried, the shrieks becoming more inhuman as each wave crashed against its monstrous form. I had tried arguing with the others who had come before. It never worked. I wasn't about to waste my breath, not when I had a job to do. This was a high-paying commission by a prestigious lord. After a while, I got used to the strange work and did what needed doing. I only had to watch as everyone drifted into the waters like a moth to a flame.

As the man reached the sea's edge with his hands held out in a comforting gesture as he tried to hush the horse, the high tide came further in, pulling him toward the screaming beast.

"Whoa! Whoa now!" the man called out before crying with pain.

The stallion rushed forward, chomping on the man's shoulder and taking a chunk of flesh. Blood soiled the churning waves as the creature twisted, knocking the man into the deep waters with a slap of its scaly, finned tail. The horse dove as the man slipped underneath, and red rushed to the surface.

I quickly dabbed my brush into a muted red hue, painting the scene before me. A hand reached out of the waters, and the horse reared, showing its complete form—half horse, half fish. It was a mermaid's steed with teeth like a piranha and a similar appetite and instinct to hunt. Perfect. It was the perfect pose. The man's face rose above water as he cried for help, the moonlight glinting off his honey-colored eyes.

I quickly sketched the silhouette with my brush, hoping to catch the scene before the feeding ended. Once again, a beautiful tale of life and death had unfolded, and I was able to capture the event. My client would undoubtedly be pleased. Sometimes, I had to wait multiple nights for my subject to arrive, but not this time. Tonight, I only waited a couple of hours.

Once the finishing touches were complete, I stood. Placing my hands on my hips, I exhaled, pleased with my work. The waves had finally subsided, as did the man's screams. The water swirled with a deadly hue. I thanked the man for his excellent show, promised that history would not forget him, and moved to the field where his horse continued to feed. I would return to town on the mount and make an extra coin by selling it.

"Thanks again, sir." I mounted the steed and looked back toward the calm ocean. "And thank you, horse."

AUGUR

This is the first chapter of my novel, Masters of the Ellem.

WHEN I was a child, an Auguress of Yiernosh visited and met with His Holiness of Byrnheilder. Her arrival had significantly been downplayed, and I thought it odd that someone held in such high esteem in one part of the world was so disrespected in another. However, as I aged, the reasoning made sense, as the Augury of the Four Sisters were masters of the Ellem and Echo-Stones, and their existence was blasphemous in the eyes of Byrnheilder's theocratic government. Surrounding the Auguress with guards would only bring unwanted attention, so her visit remained discreet to prevent conflict.

The priestess arrived on her own, armed with nothing but her Echo-Stone. I still remember the unusual purple glow that emanated from the immense charm that hung from her neck. It glistened against her black robes—a shadowy form in the dark, cloudy city—as the raindrops splashed against the ground in similar hues before disappearing in the ripples of her footsteps. The radiant stone vibrated urgently in flickering waves against her porcelain face, a face with features of a predatory animal and deep, black holes for eyes hidden beneath an even darker hood. Her mouth was set in a thin line, making her appear all the more like the nightmarish pictures depicted in my imagination from my grandmother's folktales. She was terrifying, and I hid in my room on the opposite side of my home, where I could be as far away from the eerie sight as possible. I never saw the priestess leave, but my parents told me they had watched her depart. Typically, an Auguress didn't travel to our part of the forest. The priestesshood's influence didn't extend into the nations governed by Byrnheilder, but the conflicting ideologies butted heads at the edge of Karimba Grove, just north of the Bestial Plains. Fifteen years later, I have no idea why the priestess traveled through Fiordia toward the capital, but after today's events, I wonder if she had come with a warning.

My mornings were predictable. The sound of birds awoke me, and I slugged around my kitchen for breakfast and coffee. Afterward, I tossed my thick, matted red hair into a partial ponytail, hastily braided a few strips, and secured them with decorations of feathers and beads. Makeup and frivolous clothing weren't my style, so an old, ripped blouse that showed off my stomach and a pair of frayed leather shorts with sandals were good enough for me—casual and comfortable. However, even though I lived on the city's outskirts, my typical wear wasn't well-received by proper society. Regardless of my clothing, nothing I could do would make me acceptable. I was a hybrid—a human bound by a symbiotic relationship with a fire-based Sohl. Due to this, my human features took on a more animalistic quality over the years. After smoothing my hair between my tiger-like ears and picking a piece of food out between my fangs with my long claws, I grinned at my reflection. I thought I looked fabulous. Most did not agree.

I headed to the market, a typical day that resulted in a search for fresh meat with the desire to partake in a few trades with a gangly old woman with a name I couldn't pronounce. Many accused her of being a witch. By the markings on her skin, I deduced she was from Yiernosh, but she never revealed anything about her past. She was odd and sometimes spoke in a strange language, but she was knowledgeable in the Ellem and Sohl energy and became a valuable resource regarding my understanding of nature.

While crossing the Creesis, a stretching stone bridge connecting the outside village to the main markets of Fiordia, I noticed a gathering of people and a sudden rupture of noise. Standing on my tiptoes, I tried to see what had drawn everyone's interest. A rumble shook the earth, and a deep, guttural sound came. The noise was instantly recognizable to me, though it helped that my ears were as keen as a cat's. Another howl followed, and I knew it was an Ellem. And judging by the tone and vibrating bellow, it was a big one.

I swayed to the left, my weapon at the ready on my forearm—an Ellter Brace equipped with the Sohl energy of the fire elemental I had affectionately named Tigris due to the tiger-like features engraved upon it. Narrowing my eyes, I attempted to analyze the scattered injured who lay at the opposite end of the bridge, but the dust hazed my view. Instead, I caught sight of Rondier as he leaned over my shoulder from behind to peer down at me. I nearly jumped out of my skin, seeing his face close to mine. He laughed and quickly joined my side, looking easily over the crowd.

Rondier was my best friend and an *untainted* human studying the arts of fire energy beneath me. He struggled with elemental control and had much to learn, but I trained him the best I could with my limited abilities. However, he was intelligent and picked up on things quickly. I believed in his potential. Rondier was beautiful inside and out, his dark skin and tall stature reminding me of the trees in the woods. His eyes of golden brown, green spiraling from the pupils, had a keen shimmer. Being rather boisterous, he constantly worried and lectured too much, and when he spoke, his billowing mohawk of black and red bobbed with as much vigor as his spirit. Equally, Rondier was a gentle and kind young man in his early twenties who cared way too much about everything. He never gave me any trouble for being who I was, but we had also been friends since I was a child, before my *freakish* animalistic features took over.

"What is it?" I asked him, jumping to get a better view.

"Some large Ellem…earth-powered, most likely. Appears to be out of control," he muttered, walking into the crowd. "Injured a few people, but nothing too serious yet."

I hastened after him, trying not to lose the totem pole of a man who could lift me onto his shoulders for an open view. My plan had proven unnecessary as another loud grunt echoed, followed by a violent gust of wind. After the burst, the onlookers fled the scene and took cover in the shops lining the small street. However, the old witch remained at the road's edge, her expression grim as her eyes set on the chaos. Bellowing shouts meshed with the angry roar of the massive earthen creature. It was taller than any of the neighboring structures. Stones and boulders of different shapes and sizes made up its form. Between each creaking rock was the glue of air holding it together, twisting and grinding as the creature morphed into a bull-like entity. It was an advanced Ellem that seemed even more powerful than those found in the forests of Karimba Grove. And it was at that moment that I wished I had brought Jaarha with me, even though it was frowned upon to allow wild and 'dangerous' creatures into city limits.

"Maybe we should go," Rondier said. I pretended not to hear him and continued crossing the bridge. My fingers dug into the valves of Tigris, ready to defend myself if necessary. "Don't ignore me, Keah! I know you can hear me!"

I wasn't going to back down. No one else had stepped up to take care of the feral beast. First of all, it was odd for any Ellem to lose control. It was possible that it was an adhered creature and belonged to someone, and the thing's owner hid nearby, puppeteering it as it smashed the nearby carriages and a small market storing fruits and vegetables. The question was, why would anyone want to destroy the produce?

Then I saw a flicker of black and maroon from my peripheral. The gusting air that rushed with the silhouette nearly knocked me over. With vivid, flashing light, energies of green and blue crashed against the earthen beast. Giving a noisy moan, a colossal fist of rock slammed beside the blurring shadow that danced from side to side. The shadow moved too quickly, but it was apparent it attacked the fiend, leaving me curious.

Widening my eyes, my slit pupils dilated, and I observed the aggressive action before me. I felt the familiar sense of time slow, allowing me to watch the strange being that swiped and stabbed at the rocky beast with a shimmering sword, a green glow casting from the blade. The swordsman stepped backward, dodging another angry pound from the Ellem. Twisting, he thrust the sword outward, the pointed tip embedding sharply into the rock. With bursting emerald waves, the light leaped from the blade, spiraling around the creature like a lasso. The head of the light morphed into a viperous snake, its jaw unhinging in a lively hiss as it clamped tightly onto the face of the enemy. The man pulled his sword back, and the elemental spirit of earth he possessed tightened on its own accord around the rabid Ellem. With a low grunt, the man darted forward, pressing his palm outward to summon a brilliant flash of cerulean wind energy.

Color me stunned. Never had I seen a summoner of two elements, and he could switch between the two seamlessly, was a master of both.

The tempestuous wind of the mysterious man's casting squeezed between the crevices of the rock. A low rumble quaked as the man pressed on, sending more air into the beast as the snake spirit clamped the monster tightly together. After a few more seconds, I realized the power pulsing between the crevices of the Ellem built up too much pressure against the constrictor's force. The man released the snake, calling it back to his sword, and the wind exploded outward, sending the boulders into a scattering heap with a ghastly groan that left the city silent and the bystanders in chills.

Somehow, I found myself safely behind an overturned cart with Rondier clutching my arm. The burning sting of my eyes reminded me of my intense stare, and I blinked, letting my face relax. The stranger stood in the center of the road, holding his final casting pose. Resting his weight on his front leg in a lunge, he carried his sword overhead in his right hand. The sleeve of his black robe slid to his elbow, revealing a detailed rendering of elemental tattoos, all the known types swiveling and melding together from his elbow to his wrist hidden beneath a black glove. His other arm remained straightened out, a swirling blue glow radiating from his palm. As he stood like a statue, the snake hissed from the sword's tip, its tongue flickering. Maroon leather armor fastened his dark robes together. Two flaps from his tunic hung loosely between his legs, equipped with matching leather boots. Over the tunic lay a similar leather material sewn to look like large leaves. A snakeskin belt secured the garb, and two forest-green ribbons whipped in the wind. A flicker of light caught my attention. A strange orb on his belt's center swirled emerald and blue. It lay within an engraving of a bird of prey with a snake in its clutches. I recognized this as an Echo-Stone.

The bystanders also identified the gem and the man's garments as the deathly silence erupted with gasps and murmurs. The man finally moved, sheathing his sword behind his back. I leaned to the side, staying behind the overturned cart, and tried to catch a glimpse of the man's face hidden beneath a dark hood. As if sensing my stare out of everyone else's, he glanced over his shoulder at me with black eyes. Each hair on the back of my neck stood on end as a fleeting moment passed when the stranger and I made what seemed like eye contact. I couldn't see his face as it remained hidden beneath a white porcelain mask with a bird's beak and thick feathers molded into the surface. The man was an Augur. A *male* Augur. Male Augurs supposedly didn't exist. Once again, my stubborn curiosity peaked.

In an instant, our contact broke, and he gazed upon the wreckage of the earthen Ellem that previously wreaked havoc on the town. Its broken pieces lay scattered, and the Augur pulled his palms together. At his summon, all of the debris collected, the rock crystallized, and as the dead Ellem pieced together, the random shapes took a different form. In contrast to before, when the creature seemed large and beastly, the elemental now held a more beautiful, abstract body with a face that resembled an attractive young woman. It was a rare sight as most elementals took the form of animals or nature, not humans.

At that moment, I realized this renegade Ellem consisted of both earth and air and was something else entirely—an Echo. The Augur was armed similarly, and as he stood rigidly with a lowered head, I could see his lips set into a deep frown and his jaw muscles twitching. The Echo burst into dust with a tinkling shatter and lifted upward into the clouds. A glimmer of tears slipped beneath the edge of his mask, dripping from the point of his jaw.

At a certain point in an elemental spirit's life, also known as a Sohl, the being is able to leave the weaponized vessel and live on its own accord. Usually, they are cast away in the breeze or joyfully become waves in the waters surrounding our lands. But this wasn't always the case. Some decided to take the form of living creatures, reside in the outer plains, and become Echoes. I had never seen an Echo before. Watching as the Augur shamelessly wiped away at his sharp jawline, I couldn't help but feel sadness for the foreign man as I believed it was once his Echo to command.

The streets had cleared, and many had pulled down the rattan shutters of their windows, and I remained alone, standing stupidly in awe. Well, I wasn't entirely alone. There was a constant tugging on my arm as Rondier pulled me away from the scene, shouting at me for being so careless or something of the sort. I continued watching. The Augur turned away, the crystalline dust of the dead Echo now gone, and walked toward the forest's edge.

I shouted without thought, and the man suddenly stopped, looking toward Rondier and me.

"What's your name?" I had no idea why I felt inclined to ask the mysterious man for his name, as if he would even give it to me. Augurs were heavily trained and masterful killers. He could have killed Rondier and me on the spot if he felt like it.

But he didn't.

A low, hollow sound echoed from his exposed lips. "Aegle."

Then, he was gone like a whisper in the wind.

PAPYRUS

THE BREEZE was soothing. Tiny birds sang high above on the branches. Thucydides looked up, watching the specks of light shimmering down through the plush leaves of the nearby laurel tree. The nymph, Daphne, indeed created a beautiful spectacle with this plant.

Thucydides took a deep breath, enjoying the fresh air. He had resided off the coast of Athens for days and visited the city, recording nonsense and documenting a few interesting characters he met along the way. However, the capital was crowded and not as peaceful an environment as needed to write. Because of this, he headed north toward the city of Plataea, where he sat atop one of the mountain ranges. One cliffside overlooked the town below. As he sat, he watched soldiers gather around the city's outskirts. He stared at the battle-worn armor and foreboding insignia upon their flags.

They are from Thebes, Sparta's allies. I wonder what it is they are planning to do. What about the thirty-year treaty? Has it already been broken; can they possibly be planning an attack on this great city? The Athenians best prepare themselves.' He scribbled on the papyrus at hand.

"How interesting," he muttered, feeling a new purpose rising within him. He had to document the event.

Thucydides smiled, watching the dots of people lining up in battle fashion. Was this what it was like for the eye of Zeus to look down upon his people? The man felt a sense of accomplishment at the thought and felt granted a unique sight, being the only one observing from above.

War broke out, and it was brutal and bloody. The Athenians were at a loss; their ally had betrayed them. The battle continued relentlessly until another treaty was signed only a decade later. Thucydides felt deflated, yearning for more actions to write. The writer required violence to feed his scribbling hand. He observed human nature and the soldiers' animalistic qualities and ventured from mountain top to mountain top as war broke out again, to his personal, twisted satisfaction.

Athens' soldiers lined up, ready to attack Sicily. It was ill-fated, to begin with. Many stated that the gods cursed Athens to lose. Thucydides only snorted a laugh at such petty explanations. Athens was fated to lose by their own hand—weak soldiers, inadequate battle strategies, and flawed democracy. Athens had its time in the world, and inevitably, its presence would vanish from the maps. Thucydides made sure he'd be there to account for it all.

He sat at the mountain top outside Sicily and watched the ruthless battle. Athens, as predicted, collapsed. Soldiers dropped dead by countless numbers within only seconds. Even Athena herself couldn't help the fall of the great army.

Thucydides took a deep breath, enjoying the gentle air, rustling leaves, and singing Steppe Grey Shrikes. This kind of environment was what he needed—peacefulness mixed with endless battle. He yawned, stretching sleepily. A cry of death sounded echoed within the valley. Thucydides smirked; the soldier must have received the most painful death. The superstitious would have said Ares was on the battlefield that day. There was no mercy on the playing field. The war god's bloodlust was quenched as crimson rivers matched the murky water streams. Sparta would wear the crown of the laurel that evening.

It was what he needed, indeed—harmony confined in a world of pain and misery. He'd watch the war, distanced at times to where he seemed detached from reality. The man was aware of himself as much as he was mindful of the nature of the soldiers. As long as he could form words, his writing would not cease, and as long as the battles raged on, his words would not end.

"War is a violent teacher...." the man mumbled as he reached into his bag for another stack of papyrus sheets.

QUOTE

PULSATING ELECTRIC-BLUES gave the 63rd-floor office an ethereal glow, the type of brilliance that seemed like water enveloped the entire complex—a glass prison far below the ocean waters. An occasional blur of red or green would flash, and an electric eel of traffic lights and advertisements momentarily consumed the space of the cubicle-filled room. Despite the activity of the outside world, the inside compartment remained entirely silent.

Tharin took long, slow strides, timing his movements between blinking lights so that his silhouette wouldn't strike against the reflection of the glass surrounding each workstation within the room. Like a predatory animal, he slowly breathed in and out, the air quietly passing between parted lips as he focused his energy between each silent movement, his every muscle engaged to be as stealthy as possible.

The pistol in his hand felt heavy but functioned as a certain counterbalance as he leaned around one corner, looking across the seemingly unoccupied room. He knew better. He could smell Fisher's cologne. The overpriced fragrance was the same that he always wore. Being a smoker, Fisher was oblivious to the fact that his coverage of the scent only made him an easy target.

A flash of light beamed into the room—an advertisement of white and silver introducing a new car model—nearly giving Tharin's position away. He ducked and rolled around the corner, crouching on the other side. He ran his thumb against the grooves on the slide of his silenced weapon. He unconsciously twisted the silencer, making sure everything was locked tight. With a glance, he peered at his wristwatch. If he hurried, he could make it to his favorite Chinese restaurant before it closed for the night.

A cold draft brought Tharin's attention to one of the windows on the facility's opposite end. Shards of glass covered the tiled floor from a nearby broken window. The man smirked.

'Not this time, Fisher,' he thought, not to be fooled by the diversion of scattered shards.

He could still smell him, could feel the tension in the room. Fisher was nearby. The air was thick with his fear. It was a trait Tharin had developed over the years—an understanding of the environment and an insight into the human psyche. Maybe he would've misplaced his judgment in his early years, but not today. Today, he would end this job once and for all, fairly and squarely.

A crunch of glass underfoot sounded, and Tharin rose and aimed at a nearby cubical just as Fisher sprung from one space to another, the bullet clipping his side—a stain of blood splattered against the black and white floor. Tharin frowned, already knowing it wasn't a kill-shot. He rolled his thumb across the slide again.

"J-just leave me alone, Tharin!" Fisher called out. He sounded panicked, anxious, frightened. Tharin deeply inhaled the thick air, taking in the fearful words and filling his lungs with them. This was his oxygen, his form of life.

Tharin did not reply but remained still, watching the desk that Fisher hid behind. A few thuds followed as the frightened man moved down the aisle of the dark room, hiding behind the safety of the cubicles. Tharin knew what he was up to. He was heading for his desk, where a weapon undoubtedly lay. Tharin waited patiently, glancing at his watch once again.

Fisher stood with a gun in hand and fired a blast directly at Tharin. The skilled hunter twirled around the beam he hid behind, the glass shattering in his place. He dropped to the ground and fired another shot back toward Fisher, the bullet splintering into his back as he fled from the room. Tharin gracefully pushed to his feet. He adjusted his coat sleeves, checked his pistol, and his thumb habitually pressed against the grooves again. He didn't mind the crunching glass beneath his dress shoes as he walked toward the door. Tharin eyed the red splashes of blood and came upon a pack of cigarettes. He leaned down and inspected the item. Gently shaking the box, a single cig dropped into the palm of his hand. It would be the perfect camouflage.

Staring at the large splatter on the door's paneling, he lit the item. The taste of smoke filled his lungs, and he felt one step closer to his target. The shimmering of light-play passed over the dark red through the fog of his smoke. The shot had gone abrasively through. If Fisher weren't already dead in the hall, he would be soon, and the wet trail of death would lead Tharin to his soon-to-be cold corpse.

As he rounded the corner, staring at the red, dribbled track, he thought of his favorite quote. It wasn't the character, books, or films that often utilized such a phrase that influenced his liking, but the fact that it so extensively applied to his lifestyle.

"You can run," he puffed on the cig squeezed between his teeth, "but you'll only die tired."

DINNER

MIRANDA STIRRED the pot of stew. She sniffed it and held back a gag. Meat had never been her favorite thing to eat or prepare, but it was something her husband demanded every dinner. Miranda preferred cold salads and warm soups. She liked making apple pies and treating her husband each night. But as the years passed, the woman realized that her efforts were all for naught. The man had complained about everything she did. Her food was never good enough. Despite her slight mental handicap, she worked a terrible job and paid most of the bills while he flitted from factory to factory, either getting fired or quitting for one dumb reason after another. Still, he called her names and made her feel worthless.

Miranda looked at her recipe book, slowly reaching for the salt. Maybe a bit more seasoning would help. Besides, her husband always coated everything in salt. The oven chimed, and she rushed to remove the pie she had made. It smelled strange to her, but it was a different recipe. She hoped the sugar and butter she added were enough. Sauntering back to the giant pot on the stove, she turned up the heat and added more flavor with a batch of potatoes and assorted veggies. It was their anniversary, and everything had to be perfect.

The strung-out woman had noticed that her husband returned home later and later each night over the past six months. Curious, she checked the man's phone while he was sleeping. He had a password, but he wasn't good at hiding it. Miranda had seen him enter the code countless times. That night, when he didn't arrive home until after 2 am and was drunk, she tucked him in and unlocked his phone, reading through his messages. She hid in the bathroom, crying at the unkind words he had spoken of her. He called her fat, ugly, and useless. He said his children were failures and considered them as nothing more than an inconvenience. Her husband said these things to coworkers, neighbors, and friends. He tactically twisted everything to seem like a victim while she was the monster.

Miranda was awestruck, devastated. He spoke the most to a woman he worked with—Maggie. Maggie was the cute secretary who worked in his division. She was known as the town slut, had no qualms about sleeping with the elderly business owner for an extra paycheck, and seemed to target Miranda's husband regularly. The two were quite the pair, masterminds at lying and typical narcissists. Maggie and Miranda's husband whined to each other every night for hours on end. When he was supposed to be working overtime, he was actually with the other woman. Instead of attending all the school events for their kids, he stayed with Maggie, took her on dates, and treated her better than he ever treated Miranda.

The weary wife had grown sick from reading the texts, and her tears were no longer available as she retched into the toilet. Miranda wasn't the most intelligent woman. In fact, some called her *special*, but she had a kind heart and soul. The woman would do anything for her husband and children. When she got married, most of the small town had wondered if she would be safe with a man like her husband. He seemed much older than her, creepy, disgusting, and cruel. Still, Miranda made sure everyone knew that they were in love and that nothing could ever tear them apart. So, when Miranda had read their messages, she became confused. Why would he do this to her and their family if he loved her?

"Hi, baby, how are you?"

"Rough day. Not in the mood to deal with the idiot. God, I can't wait to taste you. I'll see you at 7:00 tomorrow night?"

"Sure, babe. I can't wait. XOXO."

"It's the only thing I want for my anniversary."

Miranda couldn't read anymore, and she put the phone on her husband's nightstand and cried herself to sleep in the closet. The following day was their anniversary, and Miranda busied herself with dinner and dessert and ensured their favorite movie was ready in the DVD player. It would be the perfect evening, and her husband would have no choice but to love her more than anyone else.

Miranda poured a bit too much salt into the stew. She wailed, panicking as she tried to balance the taste with water. With every testing sip of the stew, the woman cringed. Why her husband loved things such as this was a mystery to her, but she still had to make sure it was perfect, even if it wasn't something she liked.

The front door slammed. "Oh, honey! Dinner is almost ready!" Miranda ran toward her husband, wrapping her arms around his neck. She was so happy to see him before sunset for once.

"Oh, I see."

"Are you hungry?" she asked.

"No, not really."

Miranda frowned. "Why don't you look happy? It's our anniversary! Aren't you happy?"

The man scowled. "I had an important business meeting tonight, and it got canceled. I'm not in the mood to deal with this shit."

Miranda ran to the kitchen, filling a bowl with stew. "You sit down! I-I made your favorite!" She quickly set the pot on the table, eyeing him desperately. The man rolled his eyes and sighed, dropping into his chair. "Now, you just wait. I also got your favorite beer." Miranda rushed back into the kitchen.

The man sulked in his chair, stirring the stew in his bowl. He blew on it, recognizing it was steaming hot, as his wife poured him a glass.

"It was on sale, so I bought you two cases!" she chirped.

"Yeah, great." The man ignored her as he sipped on his soup.

Miranda placed the beer beside him and rushed to the kitchen to cut him a slice of pie.

Her husband ate a spoonful of the meat and potatoes, his eyes widening. "You made this?"

"I did. Is…is it all right?" Miranda asked.

The man continued eating, not answering her. Judging by how quickly he ate, Miranda determined it meant he liked it. Her heart swelled with joy. She quickly approached the table, setting the pie beside him.

"Are you not eating?" he asked her.

She shook her head. "Nu-uh. Not right now. I'm enjoying watching you eat. Besides, I made it for you, not me."

Miranda sat at the table with her husband, admiring him as he ate her food. He cleaned his bowl, asked for seconds, and dug into the pie while she got him more. Red juice flowed over the dessert plate. The man eyed it curiously.

"What kind of pie is this? Cherry?"

Miranda laughed, bringing him more of the stew. "Oh! I guess you could call it Magpie!"

The man took a small bite, and his lips twisted. He wasn't so sure about the pie, but he loved the stew. He continued into his second bowl, alternating between both dishes.

"Magpie?" he asked as he tasted the dessert again. "I don't think I've ever had it. What kind of fruit is this?" It was tough and chewy. There was a tart, almost sour taste, but the globs of red fruit mixed with a sugary, syrupy red sauce. The crust was nice and flaky but had an unusual flavor.

"I don't know what kind of fruit it is. I dunno if you could call it fruit."

The man frowned. "Okay, what's in the pie if it's not fruit? It's strange, and I'm unsure if I like it or not."

Miranda stood, a look of terror in her eyes. "Oh, no! Did I not prepare it correctly?"

"How should I know? You won't tell me what the hell it is!"

"Magpie! It's Magpie! It's made out of Maggie! It's her fruit! It's made of the stuff you wanted to taste!" Miranda screamed.

Her husband froze, eyeing her in bewilderment. "What the hell did you just say?"

"Maggie! You said you wanted to taste her! All you wanted was to taste her for our anniversary!"

"What are you talking about?!" The man gazed upon the dishes before him in horror.

"Maggie! That woman you work with! You texted her and said you couldn't wait to taste her! Isn't this what you wanted?"

The man jumped away from the table, puking on the floor as he recognized the smell and taste of blood, realizing how much the pie resembled entrails and other unpleasant things. It all made sense to him now. He had left work, arrived at Maggie's apartment, and was sorely disappointed when she did not answer her door or respond to any messages or phone calls. He hadn't heard from the woman all day.

"What...did you do?" the man asked, vomiting again.

"Why do you love her and not me? She doesn't deserve you! I love you!" Miranda screamed. The man noticed the knife in his wife's hand as she approached him. "Eat it! You wanted it! You wanted her!"

He ran into the bathroom, slammed the door shut, and turned to find a way to escape but screamed in horror and froze in place. Blood saturated the bathroom walls. The grueling remains of what he could only assume belonged to Maggie lay in the tub. He hyperventilated to the sound of the pounding door and Miranda's screams and gagged at the sour taste in his mouth and the sight of the mutilated corpse. Everything spun as he dropped to the floor and fainted.

No one questioned what happened to Miranda's husband. Apparently, everyone knew about his affair with Maggie, and they all assumed they ran away together. That was fine and dandy with Miranda because she and the children had plenty of food to last them for months, and for the first time in her life, Miranda enjoyed the taste of meat for dinner.

TO-DO

TO-DO LIST:

1. ~~Workout~~
2. ~~Start coffee~~
3. ~~Shower~~
4. ~~Wear the skirt suit, the blue one~~
5. ~~Blonde wig~~
6. ~~Large sunglasses~~
7. ~~Eat a light breakfast—toast and eggs~~
8. Clean gun, double-check ammo

I ran the cloth over the side of my L115A3 Sniper Rifle, one of the best rifles in the world. I oiled and scrubbed the weapon before and after each use. You can never be too careful when you have a job like mine. I made sure there would be no fingerprints, no matter what. Overly cautious? Maybe. But if I were somehow, for any reason, caught before I made it to my destination, this weapon was sure not to have any evidence of my ownership.

I counted the ammunition. Never in my career had I needed to use more than two bullets, much less the five of the .388 Lapua Magnum cartridge. However, I always kept an extra mag. One would never know when things could get hairy, and I wasn't about to leave myself the possibility of being screwed during a job. As another precaution, I made my own bullets. No code, no evidence. My weapon was also wiped clean of any serial numbers and manufacturer information. An expensive modification allowed for a lighter recoil and weight, which reduced sniping distance, but I could still maintain a kill shot far from the target's location. The rifle was custom and untraceable.

I cleaned everything up, breakfast included, and loaded the parts of my weapon into my briefcase. I would piece it all together once I made it to my destination. For now, I would maintain my alias as a businesswoman.

9. 1448 S. Terrace St. Rooftop. Arrive by 14:00—prep by 14:20.

I arrived at my downtown location with plenty of time to spare. It was an old warehouse that had long been closed down and deteriorated. It smelled of rusty metal and old corn tortillas. However, the back door had remained unlocked, and a pair of wire cutters quickly gained me access to the property—I had cut the fence days prior. The grated metal stairs remained decently intact. The rooftop had the proper low walls to hide behind. I pieced together my sniper rifle, taking my time, and finished as the processional music began nearly a mile away with the faint hint of horns and drums. I aimed down the street and peered through my scope, awaiting my target. It took longer than I liked for him to take his place at the podium on the stage.

10. 14:30 extermination.

The wind picked up a bit, and I had to recalculate the shot—nothing new, simple routine. As the music faded, I waited for the applause to die down. My target arrived on stage, shook hands with a few older men in dark suits, and approached the podium to begin his speech, prewritten by some other hand that would never receive recognition.

I cleared my throat and took a deep breath as I steadied my aim. My target began speaking, and I couldn't help but grind my teeth. Sure, it was a commissioned job, one that would pay many credits. However, I couldn't deny the fact that this was a target I would have gladly offed on my own for free. But my client approached me first, and the money was too good to pass up.

Corrupt politicians and businessmen were my favorite targets, as they were often the most deserving of their early demise. Frankly, I had become annoyed that many hadn't met their end earlier. As time passed, I started taking out a few on my own time. I had enough money to live off of. Taking a few personal jobs didn't hurt, and it helped me sleep a bit better at night. And I knew today would be no different.

I took another deep breath, steadying myself once again. I couldn't quite make out his words, but I knew I had heard enough. I locked onto the fat man squabbling too close to the microphone, so much that it nearly looked suggestive as if he wanted to make love to the blasted thing. With a slow exhale, I pulled the trigger.

11. Meet Callie for dinner.

The kill shot went as planned, as it always did. As soon as I fired, I moved indoors, broke down my gun at record speed, crossed the grounds, and pulled out of the driveway before the sirens of the nearing ambulances and police vehicles were within earshot. I pulled into a local coffee shop, ordered my usual, and watched as my bank account climbed to new heights. Satisfied, I went home to change and continued with my day.

"So, did you hear the news about Halbert?" Callie asked me.

"I did," I said as I tore into a dinner roll served at our favorite restaurant.

"Crazy, isn't it?" she said with a hint of a smile.

I sipped my wine and matched her expression.

She leaned forward. "I mean, not to sound terrible, but I'm kind of glad."

I giggled but didn't say anything. I knew better, but she could read my expression well enough.

"Would you two like another glass of wine?" the waiter interrupted us.

Callie looked at me, unsure. I grinned. "Yeah. We both would like one. In fact, please bring us the whole bottle. We're celebrating."

The waiter nodded and promptly left.

"Isn't that going to be expensive?" Callie asked, looking a bit anxious.

I finished my glass, sighed, and winked at my friend. "Payday today. Don't worry. My treat."

TUNNELS

SCREAMS. ECHOED terror woke me from my slumber. Was I

asleep, or had I fainted? It was hard to tell anymore when I awoke each day

if I had fallen asleep or passed out from dehydration, illness, or fear. A searing

pain shot up my spine into the base of my skull. The scent of death and piss

invaded my nostrils, and I fought back the bile rising in my throat—a hot,

bitter acid as I had eaten little to nothing in three days. My clothing was damp

from muddy water and gore. As I patted myself down, I realized most of the

blood was not my own. However, deep lacerations traveled down my arms,

and as I twisted to rise to my feet, I felt the back of my shirt clinging to

equally sharp injuries on my back. I suppressed a cry as I tried to move.

Darkness surrounded me, and I struggled to regain my vision. I crawled

on my hands and knees, cringing as each palm pressed against slick and

mushy materials. The screams began to filter away from me, and instinct told

me to follow the sound as whatever everyone ran from undoubtedly moved

closer to me. I jogged on an uneven surface, using the wall for support, rolling

my ankles as I stepped on various slushy forms. I repeatedly fell, slathering

myself in more of the goopy mess surrounding me. The deeper into the darkness I ventured, the worse the smell got. But as long as I hurried, I kept up with the screams.

Stay in numbers. If I stay in numbers, they are less likely to catch me. If I stay quiet, I'm only helping myself. Fight back the pain. There is no time for fear or tears. Just keep moving.

I finally pushed away from the wall as my eyes adjusted. Sparingly, a flickering light lit the pathway, giving me a teasing glimpse of my surroundings. I was in an old subway tunnel. I caught up with the group's tail end, jumping into the shadows opposite one person snatched away from the light. We ran along the rail, avoiding the decrepit, decomposing corpses covering the floor. Some of the bodies appeared to be weeks, maybe months old. Some of the goo beneath our shoes was no longer recognizable as human or animal. Body parts lay strewn about, shredded, and torn to bits.

I gritted my teeth as I ran faster, moving into the middle of the fray as others were knocked down around me by humans and monsters alike. The creatures were tall, about twice the height of us. They appeared emaciated, always hungry, but nothing seemed to satiate their ravenous greed. Their form was similar to ours but nightmarish—stretched things with deep, sunken yellow eyes that reflected the blinking fluorescent lights. Their teeth were razor-sharp, holding many more than our mouths did. They had a shark-like smile, the expression permanent upon their skull-like faces. They were fast and weightlessly sprang across the platforms from one tunnel to the next, bashing people with their elongated arms.

The creatures hid during the day inside the tunnel systems. To ever journey into their nests was suicide. Judging by the number of people scurrying about, we were raided in the night and captured by a pack. Those who managed to survive the initial attack now attempted to flee. We were in their territory. And those who made too much noise attracted the monsters. I covered my mouth with my hand, quieting my heaving breaths while trying not to inhale the stench.

Left and right, enormous beings lunged into the lights, pulling people back into the darkness. Others pounced on their prey, beating them to death, blood pooling in thick, crunchy puddles. Some moved like animals on all fours, biting and clawing at those they captured. At this point, my entire body ached; I wasn't sure if I would feel anything if they caught me. The thought was morbidly tempting. I had grown tired and miserable over the past few months. Everyone I knew had died. Those who had lasted this long had turned into monsters themselves—selfish, willing to sacrifice others, violent, mad. Did I even want to survive?

I tripped over half a carcass, slipping on the mushy entrails. I gaped at the nastiness that surrounded me. The flickering light shimmered horrific glimpses of carnage—disgusting materials scattered to all edges of the tunnel system. Blood smeared along the walls. The corpses that maintained their faces held expressions of pure terror and agony. No, I did not want to die here. I did not want to be played with and torn to pieces. I pushed to my feet as one of the victims sputtered a gurgling shout. I heard the sickening pop and tear as the monster ripped through their body. It only fueled my fear. It was right beside me when it chose its victim.

The tunnel forked, half the people screeching with confusion.

"It's this way!" one man said as he pointed to the right.

"No! It's to the left! We all need to go left!" They argued. "Listen, I worked these tunnels—" One of the monsters leaped onto the man's back, its bladed teeth sinking deep into the side of his neck and shoulder.

Everyone screamed and darted to the right, stumbling through the dark tunnel. As I bounded down the rail, I saw a beam of white light shimmering at the end of the passageway. However, something blocked the trail to the top of the curved ceiling. Bodies. Gorey, mutilated, decomposing bodies piled on top of one another blocked our path. We started climbing as the screams and roars—the terrible growls—grew louder. I didn't care anymore. I climbed over the corpses, touching everything foul and rotten. As monstrous hands ripped people from the hill, I slipped between the wall and a couple of bodies, crawling in a panic—barely able to breathe—toward the opposite side. More rolled over on me, and I continued crawling between the death surrounding me. A monster lunged directly beside me through the pile, grabbing at one of those who had nearly escaped to the other side. I kept wriggling forward, my body pressing against its cold, wet skin as it maimed the person it had captured. I kept digging, pulling myself out of the mountain of decay until I fell out on the other side, rolling to the rails below.

Almost there. We were almost there. The light blinded me. I pressed forward with the very few that made it to the other side. Our footsteps echoed as we left the terrible noises behind. We exited the tunnel, and I ran directly into a chain-link fence.

"Hurry! Hurry! Open it!" someone shouted as I looked for a latch to open the gate.

Fencing covered the exit with a "no entry" sign attached to the side. The latch was also chained shut, and barbed wire lined the top, connecting to the tunnel's outside wall. There was no escape.

My fingers wrapped around the chain-link, and I shook the fence, screaming at the military vehicles that passed on the highway beside us. Panic surrounded me, and I felt sharp, slick hands latch onto my shoulders as a shrill shriek of one of the creatures rumbled in my eardrum.

HUNGER

THUNDER CRASHED, echoing against the emptiness of the dry, cracked land, rolling for eternity across the planet. Shimmers of green and electric blue danced along the horizon, tickling the edges of the sky where the clouds sank to meet the churning dust of the earth. The rumbling drone matched the moaning call of the skeletal remains that lay scattered throughout the landscape.

They couldn't hide in their skyscrapers anymore. Their underground facilities had long since caved in beneath the weight of war. Civilization remained nothing more than a ghost of shattered glass and twisted rebar. Elongated limbs reached toward the sky; scraps of clothing dangled from the shriveled and sunken flesh. Disease had set in, but still, they remained resilient. Modern medicine couldn't prevent this. Nothing could. Humanity thought itself immune to judgment and believed they were holier than the creator. Money couldn't save them. Neither could their multi-million-dollar churches, militias, or corporations. Evolution, science, religion—it all had failed them.

A boy climbed the edges of the cliffside. He was dirty, his clothing tattered but patched decently enough to protect him from the harsh climate. A few scabs decorated his skin, not from the disease but from his unforgiving travels into the Valley of the Dead. Down there, breathing made no difference. It was only a matter of time before the cold clutches of death would reach them all. The boy knew that, along with all the other children. Still, they remained steadfast and obedient, sure of their survival and unwilling to give in as the older generations had.

The boy swung a leg over the ledge, pulling himself onto the raised flat terrain. He adjusted the pack slung over his shoulder and lifted his goggles, wiping the dust from his eyes and nose. His pale irises faded from grey to icy blue as his pupils focused upon the mountainside that decorated the far skyline. A shimmering light danced along the edges of what appeared to be a peak designed as a throne. As always, he would walk to the dead tree, the only one for miles, and wait. It was common practice now, making the journey every other day. In the beginning, he would tremble with fear, sometimes cry and hide until found once again. But recent days had proven he had grown used to the death and despair encompassing his world. There was nothing to fear. It was merely another day. And days no longer held much meaning as time lost all relevance. What felt like a week was sometimes hours. What felt like hours was often days. Months had turned into years, yet he remained the same age as when the apocalypse occurred. He should have been a grown man but remained small and innocent, yet his knowledge and calm had vastly increased.

He coughed, craving a cold drink of water and the taste of freshly baked bread. The boy picked up the pace and rushed toward the tall grey tree with crooked branches. A whistle on the wind alerted him that he wouldn't have to wait long. He twisted and sank back against the trunk, pawing at the items in his sack. Current times and circumstances had brought more difficulty to his searches, but he always returned with enough to receive payment. No matter how big or small his return was, he was always adequately compensated and often generously.

The wind whistled again, this time much closer. The boy sighed, giving a slight, crooked smirk as a black mist swirled around him. It had become comforting to him. A robed figure walked from behind the tree, taking a few steps to the side to face the boy. Its gaze peered toward the edge of the cliff. A thin, skeletal hand extended from the robe and tightly gripped a staff. The accessory was far more glamorous than the figure was, made of precious metals and gems, most of which were uncommon on this plane. The haunting being turned its attention back to the boy. It looked at him with piercing white eyes sunken deep within a skull barely covered by a thin layer of skin. The hood of the robe hid most of the face in shadow. The mysterious creature was so emaciated that the gown seemed to be nothing more than a torn, dirty sheet fluttering in the wind.

"I'm hungry," the boy said.

The skeletal thing reached toward the boy, its hand supine. Without hesitation, the child handed over the sack of precious items he had picked off the dead and diseased. It did not bother to look inside but merely cinched the bag to its belt. Whatever the boy had retrieved would be enough, as it always was. With a wave of its hand, the landscape behind the tree warped, and after a quick flicker of light, a table appeared, covered with decadent cuisine. Homemade bread, warm soup, a tall glass of water, juice, and milk decorated the surface, along with platters containing various meats and cheeses. Fruit parfaits sat at the side with one unique item—a slice of chocolate cake. With a gesture, the strange being called the boy forward. Grinning, the child skipped toward the food.

"Cake?!" the boy exclaimed. He pondered for a moment, his mind calculating the days. "It's my birthday, isn't it?"

The being tilted its head and then gave a slight nod.

"You always remember!" the child laughed.

A box containing nourishment for the next few days lay underneath the table. It would get the boy through his trek down the mountain back into the valley, where he would continue his journey through the lands to find the rest of humanity's precious material items. No matter where he ended up, the cliffside appeared by the day's end, making it easy for him to reach the dead tree to hand over his goods.

As the boy finished his meal, slipping the leftover desserts into his bag, he thanked the tall creature for the food.

"I'll see you on Wednesday!" the boy said with glee. He shouldered the bag and leftovers and pressed on toward the cliff's edge. Before beginning his descent, he gave a final wave to the one who always ended his hunger.

Famine watched the child disappear and summoned a portal to return to the gates of the Kingdom, where it would bring the gifts to the mighty throne, leaving the items with all the others gathered from previous explorations. Before retreating, it gazed at the sunset, watching the blood-red orb flicker behind dusty clouds and walls of dirt. Its grip tightened around its staff. Soon, Death would take its place. Then, silence would fill these lands, and hunger would be felt no more.

MOTHER-IN-LAW

I LOVE my wife, Barbara, more than anything in the world. I cherish her. She is the most amazing, charming, and beautiful human I have ever known. And as I watch her now preparing the food for our holiday dinner, butterflies flutter in my stomach. We tease each other that it's like the baby kicking in her tummy. But I know the feeling of life in her pregnant belly must be more exhilarating. I offered a dozen times to help, but she insisted on preparing the big dinner. Barbara loves to cook. She smiles as she does it in a way that seems purer than any form of love or happiness I have seen in anyone else. I couldn't feel more blessed to have a woman like her. How on earth she came from her mother is unknown to me. Martha, Barbara's mother, is nothing more than pure hell.

"Barbara, where is that good-for-nothing man of yours?" Martha squawked. "Why isn't he the one doing the cooking? In your condition, you should be resting."

"It's okay, mother. I want to do this. I told him I didn't need any help."

"A true gentleman would do it anyway. You're about to burst. You need to sit down!"

"Mom, I love cooking. This is my favorite time to cook. Let me handle it. Here, have a glass of wine." My precious wife offered my mother-in-law a glass. I could tell that Barbara was trying to appease her. The poor thing always had to walk on eggshells whenever Martha was around. I never blamed Barbara for her mother's behavior. Thankfully, she became well accustomed to diverting her mother's negative energy toward something else. At least for a few minutes before the old hag found something else to bitch about.

"Brandon, you need to put more wood in the fireplace. It's getting cold, and you need to make sure we all stay warm," Martha demanded.

'I'd like to throw you into the fire, you old witch,' I thought.

"Brandon, I noticed the outside of the house needs repainting. Are you going to do that this spring?"

'Are you going to pay for it?'

"Brandon! How many beers have you had? This is a family event, remember."

'Remind me to spike her next glass. I'd rather have her drunk and sleepy than sober and bitchy.'

"Brandon! Help your wife, for Christ's sake! Look at her belly. She looks like she needs a nap."

'Cue another argument. I want to help my wife…if only she'd let me.'

"Brandon! Are those all the gifts you have this year? That tree is looking bare."

"Brandon! Go to the car and look for my slippers; my feet are cold and aching. When you get my age, you'll understand."

"Brandon! Tuck in your shirt. Your shoes don't match your belt."

"Brandon!"

"Brandon!"

"Brandon!"

It went on all day while my wife busied herself in the kitchen, trying her best to hide from her mother. I tolerated it because I knew how much the old woman bothered Barbara. My wife was too sweet and would never put Martha in her place. Barbara loved her mother, but I felt an unspoken, shared understanding that the old bag was also insufferable to her. For my wife and unborn child's sake, I humored the hag the best I could. But even then, nothing, no matter what, was ever good enough for Martha.

"I can't believe you are still married to him. I didn't think you'd actually marry him, let alone stay married this long. Is the baby really his? Are you sure you want to have a child with him? Any time you want to leave, you can come back home. I'll make sure you are taken care of," Martha droned as she eyed the desserts, ensuring the crusts were exactly right.

"Mom, please. You say this every time we're together. I love him, and nothing is wrong. I've never been happier," Barbara said.

"Nonsense. You were happy as a child before you met him. Before he ruined your life with marriage and children."

I held my tongue, stoking the fire. Martha's husband had left while Barbara was still a small child. It wasn't fair to Barbara, but I didn't blame the man.

"Did you feel that way when you had me?" Barbara asked.

"Never! You were the best thing that ever happened to me." Martha's voice lowered. "He doesn't deserve you! Look at you! You radiate beauty and life! You're far too pretty for him."

I sighed, grinding my teeth together. I knew I wasn't the best-looking man in the world, but come on! I wasn't *that* ugly! Wanting to pick up the pace, I made a suggestion. "Hey! Why don't we open presents now while the ham finishes baking?"

"We always wait until after we eat!" Martha protested.

"Actually," my wife chimed in, sounding exhausted. "I think that would be nice. I want to take a nap after dinner. Anymore, eating always makes me sleepy. We have a little bit of time before dinner is ready."

Unfortunately, Barbara's family was staying with us that weekend. The nieces and nephews ran around the house, wreaking havoc, but it was nice to hear laughter. Why Martha harassed me the most out of the rest of the family was unknown. Barbara was undoubtedly the prettiest girl in the family, but surely, her mother wasn't that shallow. I tossed aside the idea. Yes, Martha was that bad.

"Martha! Why don't you open yours first? Barbara got something nice for you this year!" I didn't bother trying to hide that I had nothing to do with her gift because I didn't. Nothing satisfied that witch, but if her daughter bought it, it would please her to no end, so we stopped placing my name on the gift tags.

"Well…I suppose so," Martha said, giving a low, crackling chuckle as she sat beside the fire. Barbara sat on the sofa as I played "Santa" and passed out the gifts.

"Oh, Barbara! They are so beautiful!" Martha exclaimed as she tried on her new pair of heels. For some reason, the woman had to wear heeled shoes no matter what. Even when she walked to the bathroom, she always wore her best, did her makeup and hair, and insisted that she never went anywhere while wearing slippers. She was the vainest woman I had ever known.

"I hope they aren't too tall, mother. I know they are a bit higher than you usually wear these days, but the color seemed perfect for you," Barbara said with a yawn.

"The color is just right! They match the color of my eyes, don't you think?"

Barbara nodded. "Exactly what I thought."

I continued passing out gifts. The oven dinged, and my wife finally allowed me to help. I removed the ham and carved it, and Martha watched the entire time, telling me precisely how to do it. It wasn't up to her standards, even after following her instructions. We all ate, trying to share happy stories and memories, but Martha's negativity kicked up. Everything became a sour statement, followed by something about herself—her past, age, and poor health. She did nothing but dampen the mood and suck the life out of the party. The younger kids were lucky. They got to eat in a separate dining room. We adults, however, tried to appease the nasty woman, but we all ate quickly. It was a fast meal, but it felt like hours. Finally, my wife stood from the table.

"I'm so tired. I need to rest."

Everyone complimented her on the meal. Barbara gave them a weak smile, and I quickly took the plate from her hand and placed it in the sink.

"I'll help you to bed." I guided her upstairs to our bedroom. I could tell she was exhausted, but something else bothered her. As we made it to the room, I helped her remove her shoes and change into something more comfortable. "You've exhausted yourself. You know your mother is going to blame me for this."

"I'm sorry. I just wanted to please her. She's so much to handle at times." Barbara sighed as she curled into bed. I wrapped her with a blanket and kissed her forehead. Tears rimmed her eyes, and my nerves got the best of me. "I am so tired of her, Brandon. She's negative all the time. She treats everyone so poorly. I…what if I end up like her?"

I kneeled beside the bed and kissed her knuckles as I lightly brushed her hair out of her eyes and traced my fingers along her forehead. It was a soothing gesture, and I learned that she loved it. "You will never…ever…be anything like that terrible woman."

"I pray I never become like her. I pray my children never have to endure such negativity. I'm exhausted all the time just by being around her. Her phone calls, her messages. Everything. It's…it's too much," Barbara said as she sighed, drifting into a light sleep.

I kissed her forehead. "You are so much better and so much more than that sad, bitter woman. You rest, honey. I'll take care of the cleanup."

I left the room, cracking the door just a bit so the noise downstairs didn't interrupt my wife's nap. As I did so, I heard the familiar clomping of someone coming up the stairs. I immediately knew who it was.

"Barbara?" Martha called out. She stomped to the top step, holding onto the railing for added support while wearing her brand-new pair of heels.

I blocked the top of the stairs. "She's asleep."

"Already?" the old woman asked. "I guess she wore herself out doing everything around here!"

I sighed. "She's okay, only tired. She usually does this after every meal."

"Meals that you should prepare! Do you do anything around here besides drink beer and watch TV?"

I rolled my eyes, glaring at the ceiling. "I love Barbara, and I would do anything for her."

"Yeah, right!"

"Listen, Martha. If you have a problem with me, then that's fine. But leave Barbara out of it. She needs her rest, and you've done nothing but drag her down all day," I snapped. I knew I shouldn't have said it, but I was exhausted, too, at this point.

"How dare you! I do nothing but support my child! I want nothing but the best for her! And then you came along and stole her away from me! I hoped she would open her eyes and see how much of a good-for-nothing you are, but no! You got her pregnant! I told her to abort the child, but she wouldn't listen. I told her to leave you and return home, but she wouldn't listen. What are you doing to her here? Are you abusing her? Is she too afraid to come home?" Martha ranted and raved at the top of the stairs, degrading me and my marriage, saying insane things about our unborn child and how much she hated that it was mine.

It became clear to me then that the old woman would never change. That simply because the child was mine, she would always hate it somehow. I couldn't have that. Barbara was already exhausted with how things were. She would never be able to manage her mother's abuse of her child. I couldn't take it. I wouldn't stand for it. Martha's protests grew loud, and I feared she would wake Barbara. Without another thought, I grabbed her shoulders.

"You are such a nasty, worthless bitch!" I hissed. I shoved her, probably much harder than I should have, and the woman toppled down the stairs, howling as she crunched along the way. "Oh, shit!" I let out, finally realizing what I had done.

Martha tumbled and rolled in her heels, the shoes snapping under her weight. Her fragile bones cracked against the hardwood as she twisted and slammed onto the entryway, her head banging against the stone. I rushed into the bedroom where my wife slept. I noticed she had stirred.

"It's okay, sweetie. I'll take care of it," I whispered.

Barbara hummed and fell right back asleep.

I quickly moved down the stairs, ensuring none of the kids made it to the front room. "Stay back. Just hold on. I will…call an ambulance."

Martha lay on the ground, all twisted and contorted. Someone, I wasn't sure who, asked me what had happened. I stared at her in horror, noticing her broken shoes.

"She…she fell. She came upstairs to check on Barbara, and her heel broke…and she tripped."

Silence filled the air, and nobody said a word.

TEARS

ISOBEL SAT in her tufted chair, peering out the window. It was another rainy day. Unlike everyone else, the rain soothed her. She related to the storms and felt that nature was the only thing that understood her. The tinkling of the droplets against the windowpane eased her worries. It would be another day where she would sit alone in her bedroom, avoiding everyone else in the complex. Until they needed her, that is. It had been a few days since the doctors came into her room, poking and prodding her, trying to find solutions to their never-ending questions.

She sighed, standing from her chair and lazily strolling to the vanity. She lightly brushed her ashen curls and touched her pallid cheeks. Her eyes weren't as swollen today, and her stuffy nose had finally opened enough to where she could easily breathe. She had given up long ago on making herself appear proper. Corsets, makeup, and lavish clothing were unnecessary for one who remained holed up in a bedroom nearly every moment. She glanced at the portraits lining the walls, wondering why, of everyone in her family, the disease had not taken her. She cried countless times over her lost loved ones. Some days, dealing with the pain was more manageable than others.

Isobel lazily returned to her plush pink chair, feeling the soft velvet beneath her fingertips. Sometimes, the melancholia seemed to block all her senses. Food no longer tasted good, her sense of smell had dulled, and her hands felt numb. Occasionally, she would dip her fingers in scalding water to simply feel something. She didn't care that it reddened her hands and made them swell. At the very least, the searing heat would wake up her mind, if only for a little bit.

She adjusted her white lace gown, sitting back at her desk to peer out the window. The fog had rolled in, bringing a chill with it. She wrapped a cotton shawl around her shoulders and grabbed a pen to scribble in her journal. It had been two-hundred and fifty-five days since she lost her family to illness, two-hundred and thirty-three days since the doctors began their tests, and two-hundred days since they forbade her to go outside the facility's grounds. Isobel had become a commodity of the science community. They treated her well enough and moved her into the beautiful mansion, bringing all her personal items. They fed her well, though she rarely felt hungry. The doctors were always pleasant for the most part, but sometimes they had to provoke her. Her sadness and pain were necessary for the survival of thousands.

A knock at the door distracted her writing, the sound loud and hollow within the room's silence.

"You may come in," Isobel called out in a small voice.

The door opened, and Dr. Francesca entered. "Good afternoon, Isobel. How are you feeling today?"

The young woman shrugged. "About as good as any other day."

"Any progress in your emotions?" he carefully asked. Dr. Francesca truthfully cared for the woman's wellbeing. However, they counted on her depression. It was a double-edged sword. "Any tears today?"

She shook her head. "No, I haven't cried today. Not yet, at least."

Francesca sighed. "And…your specimen jar? Have you been able to meet the required amount?"

She hung her head, her depression sinking further. "No…I'm sorry."

"I understand. And I know this means a lot to you as well. But I apologize, Isobel. We're going to need more by the end of the day. We're running out of the antidote."

Isobel looked toward him with a pitiful expression. "I feel empty inside, doctor. I have cried so much that my eyes burn. My face is red and chapped. I feel dehydrated and sick all the time. Please, is there no other way?"

Francesca kneeled beside the seated woman, patting her hand. "I feel for you, my dear. I truthfully do. I wish there were some other way. For now, all of our tests have failed. We cannot duplicate the antibodies that you create. Not yet, at least. I'm researching it day and night. I don't want you to suffer any longer, but I must ask you to keep fighting and hold on. Can you muster enough to get us through the rest of the week?"

Isobel gave a shaking breath, feeling the familiar sting of tears in her eyes. Francesca did look tired, the dark circles under his eyes aging him further. He was a bit older than her, but she found him attractive. Francesca was smart, handsome, and kind.

"I shall try my best," she whispered.

He gave her a gentle smile. "If we meet our goal for this week, I'll talk to the others and see about allowing you to go out."

She sulked. "I don't want to go anywhere alone. I'd rather stay here."

"You won't be alone. I shall go with you. And we will try out the new ice cream shop at the edge of town. I've heard plenty of good things about it."

Isobel smiled, her tears disappearing, her sadness replaced by hope. "You promise?"

"I promise," he said, sighing at his conflicted emotions. He liked seeing her happy, but he needed her to be sad. "But…one more thing."

The girl's smile faded. She knew by his expression he had terrible news.

"Your horse passed away this morning."

"What!?" Isobel's body ran cold. "Chippers is dead?"

"It seems…a pack of coyotes had gotten to him," Francesca explained.

Isobel wailed, covering her mouth. "He…got eaten? Torn apart?" She was horrified.

"I'm extremely sorry, but it seems so."

The man turned his head away as the woman screamed. Francesca stood, retrieving the glass jar on the woman's nightstand. He slowly approached her, and she hastily grabbed the container, appearing angry with him.

"I truly am sorry, Isobel. I wish it didn't seem cruel, but…" he hesitated.

"Yes, I know! My tears are necessary for the survival of many! I get it!" she snapped.

"Do you need anything else, my dear?" the man solemnly asked.

"Just leave, please. I want to be alone!"

Dr. Francesca placed a soft kiss on the top of her head before he took his leave. The gesture made the young woman pause only momentarily between her sobs. He gave her one last look before closing the door behind him, regretting that he had lied about her horse. However, they needed the antibodies, which could only come from her tears. It was a sacrifice she had to make alone, and it slowly ate away at his heart.

Isobel wailed, rubbing the edge of the jar against her cheek to catch her tears. She cried for her horse, cried for herself and her misery, for her family, and wept for Dr. Francesca, for she was in love with a married man.

PHONE

RING! RING!

I darted across the living room, slipping between my father and the old rotary telephone. I snatched up the receiver, giggling as I ignored the roll of my father's eyes.

"Hello?"

"Annette?" a smooth male voice called out from the other end.

"Hi, Robert! How are you? I've been waiting all day for your call."

Robert and I chatted every Friday night. He was only a few years older than me, had been a soldier during the war, and was originally from my hometown. We met by chance one day when he accidentally called our house phone. He had meant to call his mother, but the lines somehow kept crossing. And by the third time he called, he and I strayed into a conversation, getting to know each other better. Without fail, he called every Friday at 7:00 pm. This had gone on for months.

"So, are we still on for tomorrow night?" I asked, bobbing up and down as I twirled the phone cord around my finger.

"Yes. I do have to admit; I'm a bit nervous."

I laughed. "Yeah? What are you nervous about?"

"Well, pretty girls always make me nervous. I haven't had the chance to go on many dates, not with the war and everything."

"Pretty girls," I scoffed. "You haven't seen me yet, don't get your hopes up."

"I've heard your voice plenty, and it's the voice of a pretty lady." I could tell he was smiling by the tone of his voice. It made me blush.

"A big scary soldier, nervous about meeting a frail, little girl."

Robert chuckled. "Women always scared me more than the Nazis did."

"Hopefully, I'm not as scary as the movie we'll be watching tomorrow," I said.

A new theater occupied the downtown plaza, which was all the rage. Robert and I decided our first personal meeting should take place there. I had never been on an actual date before, so I did what all my girl friends suggested—go to a scary movie. If I got too frightened, Robert would be there to protect me. The thought of holding hands made my tummy flipflop. And then, I imagined him kissing me goodnight. I had no idea what he looked like, but I knew he would be perfect. He made me feel unlike any man had before.

"So, how will I know it's you?" I asked. "The last thing I want is to slip into the arms of the wrong Robert."

"I'll wear my dress uniform. You can't miss me."

My heart pounded. A man in uniform was always exciting!

"Sounds amazing. I will wear one of the poodle skirts my mom made. Mine is different, however. It has a cat instead of a dog."

Robert laughed. "That does not surprise me one bit."

He knew all about my love for cats. It was among the few things I could rattle about all evening. We chatted for roughly an hour before my father approached, tapping on his wristwatch.

"Ah, I got to go. Daddy's growing impatient." It always saddened me to hang up. Robert was the highlight of my week.

"All right, sweetheart. I'll see you tomorrow night."

"Right. Outside the theater, next to the payphone," I confirmed.

"Correct."

"Okay."

"Have a good night. I can't wait to see you."

"Same here. Goodnight, Robert." I hung up the phone, grinning from ear to ear.

My father shook his head. "I don't much like the idea of you spending time with a strange man tomorrow night. I know how those boys think."

"Oh, daddy! Robert is different. He's a true gentleman! He's polite and hasn't said one crude thing to me."

"Still, I want you home no later than ten o'clock tomorrow, you hear?"

I sighed and made my way to the staircase. "Yes, daddy. I know."

He turned his attention back to the television, watching the news covering the recent events surrounding Truman's presidency. I thought it was rather dull and walked upstairs to my bedroom, where I prepared for the next day.

The following afternoon was hot and humid, typical for July weather. My father dropped me off at the theater, lecturing the whole way about boys and remaining safe. He tried to up my curfew, but I protested enough to keep his previous terms.

"And how are you getting home?" he asked.

"Robert is walking me home."

"Walking? He doesn't have a car?" Dad looked rather upset by this news.

"I don't know. He suggested it, and I thought it sounded nice. Besides, it's not that far of a walk."

"Ten o'clock still stands, young lady." He shook a finger at me.

"All right, all right!" I rolled my eyes. "I'll be home by then, no matter what."

"Good. Now, have fun. And be careful!"

I waved as I trotted up the sidewalk.

"Annette!" he called out.

I sighed and looked back.

"You look nice," Dad muttered before he pulled away.

I smiled and walked toward the theater, my eyes catching the showtimes for Ghost Ship. I had heard mixed reviews, but many did say it was pretty scary. It wasn't a hit like "Singing in the Rain" had been earlier that year, but I doubted I would pay much attention to the film with Robert beside me. I waited beside the phone booth, scanning the crowd for a man in a military uniform. As time went by, I continued to grow anxious. The movie was about to begin, and Robert still hadn't shown up. I walked to the ticket holder.

"Excuse me," I started. "Has a man in a military dress uniform passed through here yet this evening?"

The woman shook her head. "Can't say I've seen anyone dressed that way tonight."

I became worried and slowly strode back toward the payphone, gazing down the sidewalks each way in the hopes of catching Robert. A moth tapped against the light post, and everything seemed extraordinarily quiet that evening. Perhaps he was running late. Maybe something terrible happened, and he couldn't make it. I eyed the payphone and suddenly realized that I didn't have his phone number. He had always been the one to call me.

"Darn it," I chewed on my nails. I was dressed in my best, had my mother help me with my makeup and hair, and now I was being stood up.

I tapped my foot and glanced at my watch. The movie was halfway through, and no man stopped to speak with me nor came out of the theater searching for me. I knew he wasn't there. I entered the phone booth in tears and called my house. It rang for a bit before someone answered.

"Hello?" It was a woman's voice.

I sniffled. "Mom?"

The line remained quiet for a moment. "Um, I'm sorry, but I think you have the wrong number."

I shook my head, stunned. "Oh, I'm sorry. I'll try again. Sorry to bother you."

"No problem, sweetheart. Goodbye."

"Bye." I hung up, dug another dime from my coin purse, and tried dialing again.

"Hello?" the same voice answered.

"Um…mom?" I hesitantly asked.

"Is this the young lady that just called?"

"Uh, yeah. I guess so. Is this the right number?" I asked as I repeated my home number.

"That's correct. This is my number. Someone must have given you the wrong number."

I shook my head in disbelief. "No, this is the number to my house. I'm trying to call my parents."

"Honey, I've owned this number for years."

"Years? We…we moved in last year. This has been our number for over a year."

The woman remained quiet a moment. "Well, that's just peculiar. You see, I've lived here most of my adult life. Lately, I've been receiving some strange phone calls. Usually, they are silent, and I can't use my phone for nearly an hour again. It's as if someone's using my phone."

I thought about Robert and how we had initially met. "Yeah. Something like that has happened to me before."

"I will have to call the phone company. I'm sure our lines have been crossed, or a duplicate was accidentally made."

"Hm, possibly. I'll also tell my parents to look into it."

"Are you all right, sweetheart?" the woman asked. "You sound a bit upset. Do you need your parents?"

"I was going to ask for a ride home, but that's all right. I don't live too far."

"At this hour? By yourself? Where are you? If it's not too far, I can give you a ride. I know that if I had a daughter, I wouldn't want her wandering the streets at night alone."

"I'm at the movie theater. It's not that far of a walk; I live on Spruce Street."

"Spruce Street?" she sounded surprised. "My goodness, I live on Spruce as well. What a strange series of events. What's your house number? I can surely give you a ride if you need it."

"425..." I spoke slowly. Things suddenly felt a bit odd, and the line fell silent. "Hello?"

"Who is this?" the woman asked with a bitter tone. "I don't appreciate prank calls."

"I...this isn't a prank call."

"I live at 425 Spruce Street! There's no way you live at this address! Who are you? Why do you kids insist on playing games with me? Has it been you all this time? Calling and staying silent on the phone? Calling and saying that you're Robert?!"

I gasped. "R-R-Robert?"

"Yes! My son! The one who died years ago! You kids have given me such grief since Robert died! Let him rest in peace! Leave me alone in peace!"

I felt dizzy. "Was...he by chance in the military? 25 years old?"

"Yes, he was! He was far too young to die! As if it wasn't bad enough to find him dead in his apartment, you kids have to call and ask for him all the time, judge me for his…his suicide!" The woman sobbed on the other end of the line while I remained frozen, trying to process the information.

"Never call this number again, you hear me?" Before I could say anything else, the woman hung up with a slam.

Stunned, I walked home alone that night. When I arrived, I told my parents about the strange phone situation and asked about the house's previous owners. Mom and Dad never had any issues with the phone. However, the house belonged to a husband and wife who had lived in the town for many years. They had one son, but he had killed himself long ago, unable to cope with the effects of the war. After receiving harassment, the previous owners packed up and moved away. Nobody had heard from them since. The following day, I went to the library and checked the past newspapers for an obituary. I found one for a young Robert, handsome as I imagined, who was pronounced dead at 7:00 pm on a Friday. After that, I never answered the phone again on Friday nights.

REHAB

HE SAT in the darkness of his room, rocking back and forth, wishing he could see the moonlight for once. They had moved him to the windowless room weeks ago once his hallucinations worsened. Initially, he went to the hospital for drug rehab, but the illusions and the events that occurred while he experienced them got him placed in the psych ward. He thought it was stupid. Moving a mentally ill person into a windowless room was a surefire way to make their illness worse, not better. Besides, he didn't have a mental illness. The shadow person was real, not a hallucination.

He shuffled uncomfortably, wishing they had at least loosened his straitjacket where he could move his shoulders enough to scratch his nose in some way. Instead, his entire torso had become numb. Flopping to the side, he rubbed his face against the wall, his bedsprings squeaking with each movement he made. The high-pitched sound reverberated in the empty room, making his ears ring. If he didn't move, his tinnitus would get worse. If anything, the facility was trying to drive him mad.

"Why do they have to use this jacket? It's not like I am the one who killed those people. I wasn't the one who scared the nurse into cardiac arrest. I didn't talk that patient into killing himself. And that incident with the needles," he looked over his shoulder at the black corner near the door, "was all your fault. Not mine."

The murky corner hummed, the edge of the room quaking in a way that only he could hear it. Vibrations traveled along the sides of the room, spiraling outward from the shadowy location. He had grown used to it by now. *It* moved through the shadows. When focusing enough, he could make out its silhouette—tall and thin, with arms that stretched to the floor, each finger pointed at the tips. If he remained quiet, his tinnitus eventually blended in with the hum of the shadow. Ultimately, the whispers started.

"I want out of this place, out of this jacket. Can you do that for me?" he asked the shadow.

The hum turned into a deep growl.

"I'm sick of this bullshit. If I'm going to be blamed for things I didn't do, I may as well have some fun. What do you say? Room check should start any minute."

The hum oscillated, responding to him.

"Yeah, if you want. As long as *they* leave me alone, you can bring your friends. They can claim whomever they want; I don't care." He hesitated. "Except for the redheaded nurse. Leave her be. She was always nice to me. Everyone else is free game."

The room groaned as if excited with the proposition. Each corner darkened, the droning sound multiplying in each direction.

"Yes, that sounds good. And the jacket. Don't forget about the jacket. It itches and smells like an armpit. I want to be able to move before we leave."

Shadows jittered along the walls, the room trembling with noise. Still, everything remained dead silent outside the chamber as the nurse approached the door.

"Okay, okay! I think he's coming. Yes, I always hold up my end of the bargain. That's how I wound up here in the first place, no thanks to you."

Keys jostled outside. With a slam, the cover over the door window slid open. The nurse looked inside, narrowing his eyes. He could see nothing in the pitch-black. "Safety check!" he called out, tapping on the glass. He unlocked the door and reached for the light switch.

Click, click.

The lights did not come on. The nurse turned on his flashlight, shining the object within the room. The patient appeared directly before him.

"Ah! Anthony! Why aren't you in bed?" the nurse cried out. Then, his body went rigid, his expression dropping into one of concern and fear. "Where is your jacket?"

Anthony smiled. "I didn't want to wear it anymore, so I asked them to remove it."

The door slammed shut behind the man. Shadows danced across the room, blocking out the light. Everything quaked, the sound booming as darkness spread over the nurse, swallowing him along with his screams.

Out in the hall, everything remained silent as the patients slept. Moonlight shimmered across the tiled floor from the barred window at the end of the building. The door to Anthony's room ruptured off its hinges as screaming shadows filled the empty corridor. A series of bangs followed as each room caved in, wispy darkness claiming the soul that inhabited each one. As the thunderous destruction filled the asylum halls, Anthony strolled toward the exit, basking in the moonlight. He noticed the redheaded nurse hiding beneath the front desk, shaking and crying.

Anthony held out his hand. "Come with me. I will keep you safe."

The woman gaped at him with fear, unmoving. She allowed him to grasp her fingers to lead her toward the exit. Finally feeling at ease for the first time in a month, Anthony slipped outdoors, taking a deep breath.

"Now, where shall we go first?" he asked as he scratched the tip of his nose.

BFF

SALLY SAT at her desk, copying the notes from the blackboard. Snickers surrounded her, and she tried to ignore the interruption as her grades were incredibly important to her. However, when a piece of paper landed on her desk, she sighed and relented to the distraction.

'Look at the weirdo. Where does she get her clothes? The funeral home?'

As Sally read it, the laughter rose in volume.

"Girls! Eyes up front! Quiet, please!" the teacher gathered their attention.

Sally slid the letter into her bookbag. She smoothed out her skirt and vest and tightened her braided ponytail before continuing with her notes; her eyes drifted to the girl sitting in the corner of the classroom. The newer student ignored everyone in the room, scribbling in her notebook. The strange child wore nothing but black with a white collar. Her hair was nearly black, but deep auburn highlights came through when the light hit it right. The girl was pale-complected and wore no makeup, which wasn't too strange as they were only in the fifth grade. However, Sally and her friends always wore makeup. The new student showed up nearly a month ago, around the time one of the other classmates had gone missing and had been brutally tortured and murdered. It took another week before anyone discovered the deceased child's head.

At lunch, Sally sat with her usual group of friends, some of the class's most intelligent and popular girls. They all came from wealthy families and wore expensive, clean clothing. Sally opened her lunchbox and was glad to see a sushi and fruit salad pairing. Her mother always spoiled her with food. She was never allowed to eat the trash the cafeteria served.

"I bet she did it," one of Sally's friends said.

"Who?"

"Her," the girl pointed toward the new student. "I bet she was the one who killed Rebecca."

The table's occupants rumbled with giggles and whispers. Sally peered at the black-clad child and huffed a sigh.

"I doubt it," she said as she rolled her eyes. She stood and closed her lunchbox.

"Where are you going?"

"I'm gonna go talk to her," Sally replied.

"Are you crazy!? Look at her! I bet she's a witch!"

Sally ignored her friends' remarks and approached the lonely girl sitting alone in the cafeteria's center.

"Hi!" Sally chimed. "Can I sit with you?"

The girl gaped at her with wide eyes. "Uh…sure," she replied with a tiny voice.

Sally grinned and dropped into the seat across from the other girl. "I'm Sally. What was your name again?"

"…Candice," the pale child replied.

"Candice. That's a pretty name. Say, Candice, have you ever tried sushi?"

Candice shook her head 'no.'

"Would you like to try some? Mom always packs way too much, so I can share if you'd like. The cafeteria food isn't all that great."

For the first time, Sally saw Candice smile. "It isn't very good food. I forgot to bring my lunch this morning," the shy child replied.

Sally shoved her lunchbox into the center of the table. "Then, have as much as you like!"

Sally shared her lunch and swung with Candice on the playground that day, and they walked home together once she found out that Candice lived close to her. These activities became a trend that lasted for weeks. The new student came out of her shell. She didn't hide beneath her hair like she used to. Her grades improved. The others had finally accepted her to sit with them at the same table. Eventually, Candice stayed at Sally's to do homework and watch TV.

"Can I tell you something?" Candice spoke up one afternoon as they watched cartoons and finished their math homework.

"Like…a secret?" Sally asked, his face lighting up with interest.

"Yeah…kinda."

Sally set her soda to the side and leaned forward, peering at her friend with interest. "Well? Go on!"

Candice drank from her soda can and eyed the TV to avoid eye contact. "I've…never had a real friend before."

"Really?!" Sally asked. "But…but you're so wonderful and nice!"

Candice lowered her head. "My family moves a lot, so I never could make any good friends."

Sally reached around Candice and hugged her. "Well, you know what?"

"What?"

"You can be *MY* friend. Forever and always! My BFF!" Sally cheered.

Candice looked over the other girl's blonde hair and blue eyes. What a pair the two made with their contrasting looks. After a second, Candice's face lit up. "BFFs?"

"BFFs!" Sally bobbed her head. "Best friends forever!"

The two giggled and moved closer to one another, finishing their afternoon programs. Once dinner was about to be served, Sally walked Candice home. As they passed by the slough, which ran along the edge of town, Sally hopped across the sidewalk to the water's edge.

"Hey, do you wanna know about one of my secrets?" Sally asked.

Candice followed her.

"You know, since you told me about one of yours? It's only fair, and I want to be a good friend. Friends don't keep any secrets from each other, right?" Sally walked to the tree line.

"Okay, sure!" Candice crawled over a log.

Sally skipped, excited that Candice was interested in her secret. "Great! You can't tell anyone! Okay?! I found this really cool place…in the trees. I don't think anyone knows about it."

"Sounds scary," Candice said. "Show me!"

Sally giggled and led the way deep into the wooded area.

"So, what is it?" the other girl asked.

"Well, a long time ago, I heard a rumor that a crazy lady once lived out here. She was banned from the town and sent out here to live in solitude. Soon after, children started disappearing." Sally pushed through some low-hanging branches and came into a clearing. A dilapidated house sat in the clearing, hidden behind overgrown brush and trees. "See!? I found it!"

Candice gaped at the house in awe. It was tiny, but someone could have lived there once. "That place is undoubtedly haunted."

Sally twirled around, her hands behind her back as she smiled, a sweet expression before the ghastly scene behind her. "Pretty cool, huh? Come on!"

"Wait! You're going in?"

"Duh! It's really cool!" Sally rushed inside.

Candice shivered as she eyed the house. She liked scary movies and video games; however, standing before a real haunted house made her uneasy. She yelped as she crossed through the entry, brushing a spindly spider off her shoulder. She stumbled into a table of various utensils and backed into the corner of one wall. Despite the daylight, it remained dark inside.

"Sally?" she whispered. "Where did you go?"

"Right here!" Sally said as she turned on an oil lamp on the opposite side of the room.

Candice gasped and covered her mouth. The smell finally hit her, and she felt nauseous. Animal skins lined the wall. The bloody, fleshy carcasses filled the sink and countertops. They were slaughtered in cruel and sickening ways. Some were rotten; others were pieced together to create mixed-breed monsters. Candice swayed and ran for the door. Sally beat her to it, covering the exit.

"Woah, woah! Wait! It's okay! It's okay!" Sally reassured her.

"Sally…what the heck is this? This is disgusting! I'm going to throw up! Someone lives here, and they are doing…" she gaped at the horror around her again, "terrible things. We need to tell somebody."

"No!" Sally screamed with a stomp. "This is my secret, and we aren't telling anybody!"

Candice stepped back, her eyes drifting to the carcasses and the other child. "You…did you do this?"

"I showed my other friend this, and she freaked out, too! After everything we had been through, she got mad at me and called me names. She threatened to tell our parents!" Sally walked toward the table, her fingers trailing over the bloody utensils.

"Your…your friend?" Candice slowly walked back to the opposite side of the room, close to a broken window.

"Yeah," Sally bitterly responded. "Rebecca. You may have heard about her."

Candice looked confused, shaking her head.

"The girl they found dead last month," Sally rolled her eyes. "You know…animals are one thing, but humans are completely different. I'm not sure if I would ever want to do that again."

"Do what, Sally?" Candice said, tears stinging her eyes. Her heart thumped wildly, a deafening beat in her ears.

"She was going to tell everyone! Do you know how angry my mother would be? Do you know how scary my mom is when she is mad?!" Sally shrieked as she grabbed a knife and continuously stabbed one of the dead creatures beside her. "Do…you…know…why…I…wear…so…much …makeup?" she asked, each word spoken between stabs.

Candice watched in horror as the girl licked the palm of her hand, wiped it across her face, and frantically wiped off her makeup with her shirt. Bruises covered Sally's cheeks, and blackness smudged beneath one eye. A scar lined the bridge of her nose. The blonde girl opened her mouth and promptly pulled out a row of teeth. She wore removable veneers. Sally cried, leaning against the table.

"I hate her! I hate her!" she screamed.

Candice's nerves calmed somewhat, and she suddenly pitied the girl.

Sobbing uncontrollably, Sally gestured toward the corpses. "I…I don't mean to. I just…I get so angry! And Rebecca! She-she used to be so mean to me. I just wanted her to be my friend, to be nice to me. And when she saw this, she called me so many names. She called me crazy and psycho." Sally slipped her teeth back into her mouth. "I couldn't let her tell my mom."

Candice took a deep, slow breath. "I…won't tell your mom."

Sally quickly fell silent, looking toward the other child. "You…you won't?"

Candice walked toward the table, eyeing the bloody tools. "No, but…" she lifted one of the knives, "I think we should show her this place." Candice grinned. "Besides, what are BFFs for?"

UNWRITTEN

DEATH IS a subject that many don't like to talk about. Why don't we speak to our loved ones while on their deathbed? Not about the small things. Why don't we ask the important questions? Not just the "how are you feeling" questions but the more profound, darker subjects.

"Does it hurt? Are you cold or hot? Do you see anything…different? Do you hear the voices of angels? What are your dreams like? Are you afraid or happy to go? What do you regret? What is your happiest memory? Worst memory? If you had more time, what would you do?"

Interviewing the dying would be incredibly helpful to the rest of us. By questioning everyone during this time of our life cycle, perhaps we could gain more knowledge and evidence of the paranormal and spirituality—prove or disprove religious beliefs.

"Does it hurt?"

Well, it depends on the situation. For many of us, we end up sick, hospitalized, diseased, or full of cancer. Some of us are fatally wounded or injured, suffering for days or weeks before passing. Others are luckier, moving on in their sleep or instantly. Sometimes, an accidental death may seem horrific, but we should be thankful for those who die immediately without feeling a thing. For me, it hurts. The aches and pains are too much, but sometimes I feel numb to it. You do, and you don't get used to it. You learn to tolerate it more as time passes.

"Are you cold or hot?"

Cold. I think most of us feel cold. Our life force is leaving our bodies. Now, for those who feel warm, it could be fever or infection. It could be that they are hallucinating about the bowels of Hell opening up beneath them. It all depends on the person and what they are dealing with. Sometimes, it hangs on their own religious beliefs and guilt.

"Do you see anything…different?"

Many in my position start to see things differently all around us. For one, I notice more of the tiny details—how a person smiles, the sadness in their eyes. I can tell everyone surrounding me is either sad or scared, and for some reason, that gives me strength. I must be strong for them. As for "different," I've seen and heard a few unnatural things, yes.

"Do you hear the voices of angels?"

The woman in the room next to me used to. She said she could hear them singing when she went to sleep at night. It lasted a few days before she went into a coma and became brain-dead soon after. Though I have not heard the voices of angels, the fact that she had is comforting. I'll know my end is near if I hear singing when I fall asleep. However, I sometimes hear the voices of friends and family who have long since passed. Usually, it is only their voice saying my name and not much more. The doctors tell me it's the morphine. I don't entirely believe them.

"What are your dreams like?"

They haven't changed much since I was hospitalized. But now and then, I dream of getting out of bed feeling young and healthy again. I've dreamt of events from when I was younger or conversations with my parents. Many say it's because I have death on my mind. It's possible, but sometimes the discussions and imagery are comforting, so I find the meaning behind them. Anymore, I'd rather have dreams like that than any other.

"Are you happy or afraid to go?"

I used to fear death. But anymore, I will be glad for my suffering to end. My life wasn't the happiest or healthiest. I endured many hardships—abusive relationships, horrible career choices, and health issues. I'm not much afraid anymore. And I'm not as happy as I am at peace with the idea of leaving this world. I hope that whatever awaits me after death will be pleasant and peaceful. I certainly don't want to be one of those who die screaming, seeing shadows and flames crawling up the walls. No, I'd much rather hear the voices of angels.

"What do you regret?"

I regret trying to grow up too fast. I rushed out of high school, and my youth was stolen by marriage. I never had much chance to enjoy my life before becoming a mother. Never will I ever regret my children. I regret not taking risks and doing more for myself and my happiness. I regret not kissing that boy in college. I regret not leaving my first husband sooner, for my sake and the kids.' I regret not eating all the damn pizza and ice cream I wanted. I was diseased and sick, to begin with; a bit of tasty food would not have hurt much. Besides, losing weight and maintaining a perfect image for a man was not worth it. No man ever tasted or felt as good as a pizza, that's for damn sure.

"What is your happiest memory?"

My happiest memories are of the holidays. I grew up making cookies and candies with my grandmother until adulthood. I missed those traditions. But once I had children and then grandchildren of my own, I continued those traditions. There's something nostalgic and calming about baking while sipping on cider—sometimes with a touch of rum added—while listening to

Christmas music and children's laughter. I am pleased that the tradition will not die with me.

"Your worst memory?"

My worst memories always center around my life with my ex-husband. His abuse, mentally and physically, took a toll on my health. I remained on medication to cope with the past throughout the remainder of my life. And to make it worse, it wasn't just me he affected, but my babies as well. That will always be my biggest regret and worst memory.

"If you had more time, what would you do?"

Probably write this all down—in a notebook, as a poem, in a book. Anything to let people know what it's like to lay on your deathbed. To understand what not to take for granted. I could say the stereotypical thing— to enjoy the time with family, and it's the little things that count. Chase after your dreams and never do anything you would later regret. Do the things that you will regret not doing. There is only one life; do the deed. There is only one life; love yourself and as many others as possible. Time is short, and all of this is true, but one simply does not understand until their time is up.

I have pondered these things repeatedly, waiting for the clock to stop on my lifeline. I no longer have the use of my hands. I can barely speak, let alone write. As the room brightened around me and I saw the tall shadow approaching the bed's side, I smiled. The only thing I regret is that my final thoughts and advice were left unwritten.

THE LAW

"BRING IN offender #27356." The corrections officer flipped through the pages on her clipboard.

The door to the sterile white room opened, and a man entered under another female officer's escort. Nervous, the prisoner fidgeted with his cuffs, the chains rattling together as the woman led him toward the reclining bleached leather chair in the center of the room.

"Hello, Gerald," the officer with the clipboard greeted. Gerald did not respond but took slow, even breaths. "This is your sixth offense. You know what that means?" He finally met her green eyes. Her blonde hair was pulled into a tight bun, accentuating the arch of her eyebrows.

"It wasn't my fault. I couldn't help it. He made me look," Gerald spoke up, tearing his gaze away from the woman. "It was my roommate's fault."

"It was only a matter of time," the blonde officer said as she sat on a stool beside the chair Gerald occupied. Next to them stood a metal table, much like those found in surgical rooms. A large, round, metallic device lay atop it with two needles protruding from the inner ring. "You will be released today, but you must wear the ring. You will be put under house arrest for a month."

"What about Ron?" Gerald asked as they cuffed him to the chair. The officer who brought him into the room moved toward the door, keeping guard. A nurse knocked and entered the room.

The blonde officer plugged into a small device wrapped around Gerald's wrist. "He, too, will be put under house arrest. His ring has been recalibrated. You know his time is minimal, so I suggest the two of you behave." His vitals appeared on a monitor beside them, calculating every strike against his previous offenses.

"You can't possibly make me stay with that pervert for a month! He deliberately makes me look at things…to create impure thoughts. He's sick and twisted! I don't know how his God's Eye hasn't deactivated him yet," Gerald protested.

"Maybe you should have thought about that before you decided to move in with him. You were aware of Ron's previous major offenses." The officer stood, gathering up the metallic loop. "Let's get this over with. I have many to deal with today."

The lab technician took a wet swab and wiped down Gerald's temples. The officer read through the paperwork as the specialist prepped the prisoner for the God's Eye ring.

"Gerald, after every thousand counts of impure thoughts, you are met with jail time, but you must be equipped with the God's Eye ring by the sixth major offense. The ring will continue to calibrate and filter your thoughts. Any feelings deemed impure by the device—sexual, violent, racial, offensive—will be counted as a strike toward your final offense. The ring will detonate by your seventh major offense, deactivating your cerebral core." The officer leaned forward. Gerald tried his best not to look at her red-painted lips or the way her suit hugged around her curves. The counter on the monitor blipped, and the officer scowled. "Disgusting. Your life is in your own hands."

"But it's not fair!" Gerald gave a half-hearted sob.

"It's the law. We all follow the same rules, Gerald."

The man squirmed in his chair. "Is it gonna hurt?" he asked.

The nurse hummed a bit. "Hmm, you'll feel a pinch, but nothing intolerable."

As the officer held onto the device for added support, the nurse gently sank the needles into the man's temporal lobes. He clenched his teeth, arching his back, groaning. The women surrounding him remained unsympathetic. Gerald was a liar, a known abuser, and a sexual offender. The counter never lied, and the man had a plethora of impure thoughts every hour of every day. Once the procedure had finished, the man was given two painkillers and sent back onto the streets, where a bus deposited him at the front door of his deplorable apartment complex. Every person he passed gave him a wary look. His ring revealed to those around him his crimes and offenses. He wore his sentence like a badge to serve as a warning to everyone who dared to follow in his footsteps.

Gerald quickly climbed the stairs to his apartment, fumbling with his keys. He had only a few minutes left to get into his home, or the device would notify the authorities. As he entered the tiny abode, he fought back the rising bile in his throat. His head throbbed with a type of pain he had never felt before.

"Just a pinch, my ass," the man grumbled, searching for his vodka and more painkillers.

"Gerald!" A voice shouted, making the man wince.

"Goddamnit! Don't shout!" Gerald swallowed back a handful of pills, glaring at his roommate. Ron stumbled into the room, clearly drunk or high or a mixture of both.

"We're like twins now!" Ron laughed, his eyes bugging out as he pointed at the ring on his head.

"Yeah, fantastic."

"Come 'ere! I wanna show you something!" Ron motioned for Gerald to follow.

"I ain't going anywhere near your bedroom. You've already fucked me over enough."

"No, no! I promise it'll be good! I swear! You'll wanna see this!" Ron hopped a little bit, trying to coax Gerald into obeying.

"No." Gerald stomped toward his bedroom while Ron giggled, following. If he didn't know better, he'd say Ron already suffered from brain damage. "Why are you following me?"

"No reason! No reason!" Ron snickered.

Gerald stumbled against the wall, vomiting. "Goddamnit."

"You're going to blackout! I did the same thing! Don't worry; you'll wake up soon," Ron said as he poked Gerald with his finger, laughing maniacally.

By the time Gerald regained consciousness, it was already dark outside. His head lolled to the side as his stomach churned. His vision blurred, and he found that he sat in a chair in a dark room; the stench of rotten food and sweat overwhelmed his senses. He tried to stand but found himself strapped in place.

"What on earth?" he mumbled.

A monitor clicked on in front of him, flashing a loud pornographic film. Gerald tried to look away, cursing as he fought with his bindings.

"Look, look! We haven't seen anything like this one yet!" Ron giggled.

The insane man sat on the bed of his filthy room, eating a bag of chips.

"Ron! What are you doing?! Are you mental?! You're going to get us killed!"

"Yes, yes! And what better way can we go out?" Ron laughed and unzipped his pants.

Gerald struggled to find a dark place to focus on within the room. His thoughts alternated between interest in the videos that Ron forced him to watch and the desire to kill his roommate. He struggled, but after an hour, his counter continued to rise. He felt sick as his roommate pleasured himself, saying crude and repulsive things.

"I hate you! I will kill you when I get out of this chair!" Gerald tugged, trying to release himself from the plastic zip ties.

A loud beep sounded from where Ron occupied the bed. He gave a crazed laugh, and a sickening pop erupted. Gerald grimaced, looking over his shoulder the best he could to see his dead roommate flopped over the side of the bed, blood dripping onto the floor.

"You sick fuck! You twisted bastard! I hate you! I am glad you're dead! You mother fucker!" Gerald screamed. "Somebody get me out of here!"

Gerald fought. The zip ties cut into his skin, the metal chair wouldn't budge even with his strength, he had to remain under house arrest for a month, and now Ron was dead. Nobody would become suspicious if he never left the house. Nobody in the apartment complex would respond to his screams. Realization sank in as Gerald stared at the monitor before him, the display flashing a multitude of never-ending sexual content.

A small laugh passed his lips. "Heh…fuck you, Ron." He gave in, listening to the quickening clicks of his God's Eye counter.

JANUARY

WALKING LONG strides, adjusting his tie, the tall Russian man approached the Spymistress, standing firm before her desk. She gave him an expectant look yet remained silent as he dropped the file upon the wooden top. The elite woman wore her typical blue dress suit, had her nails and hair in impeccable condition, and seemed far from the woman he would place in charge of such an elaborate position within British Intelligence. However, he knew better than to judge someone by their looks. He could tell she was knowledgeable and dangerous by the look in her eyes and how she fed him a sly smile as she pawed the folder, dragging it across the modern desk.

He looked to the side as she flicked through the pages, noting the photographs contained within the document. The room was situated underground, with screens lining the walls to give the illusion of being on a high-rise. White light flooded from the edges of the substitute windows, illuminating the room with a healthy glow. The man remained rigid as the Mistress read, risking a light touch to his bruised cheek.

"Rough night?" she asked, her warm voice invading the silence.

"You could say that."

"Janus, where is Gregory?" She lowered the paperwork and eyed him with a grave expression. "I've heard rumors."

Janus cleared his throat. "The throwaway became just that…thrown away."

The mistress glared. "I'd prefer all our agents to survive the mission, Janus. And I prefer the term discard, not throwaway. Gregory was meant to be arrested as a means to protect your identity."

"Right. And he was."

"He was killed in the process."

"Mistress, things were getting out of hand. I believe he was working as a double agent for Russian Intelligence. He knew a bit too much for my liking. Was he made aware that I was a defector?"

"Your identity has been kept secret from the other agents once you came to us. Now you are saying that our Floater agent has been working for Russian Intelligence this entire time? What would be the odds of two double agents working on a case together?" Mistress eyed the file again, awaiting a logical explanation. "We have his legend, and everything checked out when we decided to use him."

"Page six, Mistress. All the bona fides are there. He once operated as a honey trap for Russian intelligence to work through the British elites and government officials. He's been their Raven for the past four years," Janus coldly explained.

"This makes no sense. How could we have missed all of this?" Mistress eyed the pages with confusion. "There's absolutely no evidence until today that Gregory was a double agent. Are you positive that these documents have come from a reliable source?"

"Captured the data myself. Gregory may have worked within the Russian loop for a few years, but I was raised within the system. I know the ins and outs of that organization. If I allowed him to be arrested, he would have spilled the news of my working with you against Russia, blowing our entire operation. Therefore, I had to be sure he never spoke of my existence or knowledge of my collaboration with Britain. If I ever go back to Russia and get caught, I'm a dead man. And we both know that would not only be sorrowful for me, but you'll also lose your greatest asset to this war."

"Cheeky bastard. Next time you go out, I'm sending you with a friendly birdwatcher. I expect you both to return alive or within the mission requirements."

"Babysitting another agent will only be a distraction for me."

"No, the babysitter is for you. Every mission so far has been mucked up in some way. You're sloppy. You've nearly compromised your partners every time. I'm giving you one last chance to prove yourself tonight. If anything gets cocked up, the slightest misstep, I will have eyes on you. You have more than your old allies to worry about."

Janus swallowed hard, giving a harsh sigh.

"Am I understood?" she sternly asked.

"Yes, ma'am."

"Now, what disinformation was given to Russian intelligence?" she changed the subject.

Janus gave a detailed brief about the incorrect information in Russia's hands.

Initially, Russian intelligence sent him as a Dangle for recruitment to gather information. However, Janus fully defected and now worked against his country, feeding his original agency false information for the Brits' benefit.

That night, there was to be a General Assembly at the United Nations. Janus' informant had stated that Russia was planning to target Pakistan's leader, pinning evidence against the Brits. However, Janus used the same information but flipped the nations for the information given to Russia.

Despite the threats, the meeting commenced while under tight security. Pakistan's leader avoided appearing in person but had another take his place as the rumors spread throughout the nations. British intelligence sent their elite teams to keep watch over the UN Headquarters in New York and the Pakistani leader's home. The Russians did the same as planned, creating secret assassinations and mini-battles amongst the teams, all set up by the information that Janus had propagated between the two nations.

Janus' phone rang as he watched the news in his small, empty apartment. He wordlessly answered it. "Agent January," an American spoke over the line. "Both agencies have been infiltrated. The information you gave us has been proven true. All missions and agents for the two nations have now been compromised. If you look outside your door, a drop has been made. You will find your papers, identification, and new banking information inside. America thanks you for your cooperation. Keep this cell device, as we may need your services in the future."

January opened his apartment door and retrieved the package. It contained all the specified materials. "Package received." He looked up the bank account data and smiled at the seven figures. "Thank you, sir."

"Thank you, Agent January. Oh, and welcome to America."

PARADISE

CRYSTALLINE WALLS and walkways—paths with the essence of magic.

Enormous arches and gilded stained-glass windows—entries to places of wonder.

Stretching bridges of marble and silver connected the Gothic towers.

Ives was a paradise encircled by bulbous clouds and narrow waterfalls.

No space went without a splendorous view.

There was not a soul who went without the reach of a quiet space to themselves.

The breeze carried gentle songs as chimes jingled from countless sources,

From the Emerald musicians to the church chambers, where the early morning rituals took place.

Everyone respected and loved one another and nodded as they passed by.

It was a paradise, indeed.

A place of serenity.

A place of infinite joy.

Every soul had a gift.

Everyone had a passion.

They practiced their daily worship with ease and without a second thought.

They had a routine, a disciplined structure.

Tiny bluebirds chirped quietly in the trees, flitting from the branches which carried orchids and fruit.

Red and yellow fish swam happily within the garden pools, eating lightning bugs hovering above the surface.

It was an extravagant sight that awed all manner of beings who entered.

The land remained protected for over five thousand years, secluded from other societies.

They were a genius race, masters of science, the arts, and illusion.

Whenever conflict erupted, they refused to take a side, remaining neutral unless necessary,

Though they had the power to stop a hundred wars within minutes with their abilities.

Peace and love were their preferred way of life.

But as centuries passed, they weakened, forgetting their purpose of protecting humanity.

An ambush arrived at their doorstep, bringing with it deadly turmoil.

A kingdom of five millennia fell in minutes.

Now, the walls are no longer spotless marble but ashen tombs.

There are no more precious materials decorating the archaic surfaces.

There is no more laughter, no more joy.

All that's left is ruin,

The ruins of a once-mighty race,

Remnants that are far forgotten with no textbooks to tell about them,

Shambles where only souls reside, woeful, full of animosity, rage, and regret.

One soul, in particular, never let go.

He still clings to life like he has a purpose.

This miserable being stands watch over the sacred land for all eternity to wash his hands of sin,

To spend all time without happiness, without love, and with no forgiveness.

This is what remains of the once-great race,

A race that should have remained immortal,

A race that died by their own hand.

The Feral closed his diary, tucked away his pen, and watched from a great distance as the lone survivor of the cursed race scoured the earth. For what? he didn't know. Perhaps the survivor searched for life, for a lingering reminder of his past, a friend in the lizards that scampered among the fields and deserts, or maybe it was a mindless journey. Either way, it was a melancholic display. The survivor moaned a heart-wrenching melody of tears, a sound that normal ears would not hear, just like regular sight would not perceive from this location. The Feral kept his distance. Since birth, he and his kind strayed away from civilization. They were too dangerous, too abnormal to interact with the others who came from the heavens, let alone humanity.

No, he would watch as the survivor swooped and hovered in the air, his giant wings creating gales that tickled the edges of the forest's trees and added ripples to the silvery lakes. The Feral debated calling out and traversing the landscape to meet the lonely soul. However, the toxicity of his mere presence would prove deadly to the one who had already endured so much pain. No, this was for the better. The Feral had lost all of his kind in the fatal blast that ruptured through the small continent. His radioactive body absorbed most of the impact and ricocheted the rest, further adding to the destruction. His mere existence was deadly, lonely, and miserable. And for a moment, he felt relief that he was not utterly alone in his suffering. For now, the two inhabitants of the land were twin souls, sharing in everlasting pain.

But he pondered, perhaps he should visit the survivor. Wouldn't he be granting the poor soul some mercy even upon the chance of death? The Feral could quickly end the other's existence. But then, what about himself? He would suffer alone, but that was also a selfish thought. Still, the Feral lived by a strict moral code. Merciful or not, killing someone was wrong, even if the one soaring above with weeping sadness was to blame for so many deaths. Revenge or compassion, neither one seemed to befit the motion of acting on murder.

"No. There is certainly a plan for you, and it is one I can see much clearer than my own," the Feral spoke softly, his words trailing on the open breeze.

For now, he would venture to his hiding place among the forests and waterfalls on the eastern shore. And when his time would come, as his earthly form became further unstable, he would dive one last time from the tallest cliff out into the deepest depths of the ocean, where his body could expire in the safest way possible. The amount of radioactivity his existence held was enough to destroy any evidence of the holy land and more. And he had no intention of destroying something so treacherously heartbreaking and beautiful.

"Farewell, my lost friend, the lone survivor of these lands. I know not how much longer I have, but I wish only the best for you and the safest of journeys. I hope you realize that despite all your aches, you are not alone, even when no one returns your call or reveals themselves from the shadows of this world. I take comfort in your existence and hope you can feel the same relief someday."

The Feral turned away as the gliding dot on the horizon trailed into a gathering of clouds. He would never see the survivor again. And the survivor would never know of his existence.

FIRE

THUMP.

The heavy briefcase carelessly dropped onto the floor, and a flutter of dusty ash drifted into the air, clinging to the sides of the black casing. The detective placed her hands on her hips, glancing at the filthy room. A low hum passed her lips as she contemplated her surroundings.

"Morning, Ilayda," a male voice greeted.

"Hey, Zarek," Ilayda said with an exhausted sigh. She investigated the scene—a small apartment burnt nearly unrecognizable on the complex's top floor.

"Well, what do you think?" Zarek chimed in, brushing off his black jacket, which seemed a magnificent dust magnet.

"Seems like a typical pyromaniac." Ilayda shrugged as she strolled into the kitchen. Nothing lay on the stove; in fact, the top surface seemed less burned than the rest of the house. "Didn't start in the kitchen," she stated the obvious and returned to the living room, lightly stepping over a large pile of ash and down the hall into the bedroom. The bed was utterly destroyed, the mattress demolished into nothing more than a few crusty springs among a filthy mound. The bathroom seemed practically undamaged. Giving a sound humph, she twirled on the balls of her feet to look at her partner. "Okay, I thought this was a murder investigation."

"It is," Zarek stated; a slight smirk crossed his delicate features.

"So…where is the body?"

Zarek pointed. Following his finger, she turned around the corner into the living room. Her eyes trailed down the wall to a large pile of ash she had previously stepped over. "This?" she asked.

"It's the only conclusion I could come up with."

"That's impossible." She shook her head. The amount of time and heat required to dissolve a person into nothing more than a pile of ash was a bit longer than what it took to call in the fire and have it put out. It was unnecessary, as the fire had already subsided once authorities arrived.

"I was thinking the same thing. Usually, you get charred bodies." Zarek stepped forward to meet the woman's side. She twirled her russet hair with a finger, her mouth twisting to the side.

"Or at least some bones or teeth." She kneeled, poking the end of her pen into the dusty pile. It was soft, with no lumps. "Are you sure there was someone in this apartment? Maybe this was a pile of…paper or something."

"Well, that's what I'd guess, too, except that people heard screaming before the incident occurred. They also took some samples to the lab. We should know soon."

Ilayda turned her head, looking at the toppled chair beside the window. "Possible signs of foul play."

"He either came in from the window or the rooftop, where there are no cameras, but that would require the victim to allow the perpetrator inside." The man added, "Unless it was someone who had a key to the place."

"You know what I don't get?" Ilayda rose to her feet; her emerald eyes shimmered in the morning light that flooded in from the nearby window.

Specks of ash glittered as they danced through the air. "Wasn't most of the building consumed by the fire?"

"There were multiple phone calls throughout the night. It seems twenty cases of fires were reported in this building alone. Luckily, the complex is undergoing major renovations, and many residents have relocated to a nearby facility. However," the man paused, looking at the small memo pad in his hand, "it seems many of the current residents were consumed in the fire. Some had managed to get out safely after noticing the other burning apartments. About forty deaths total last night."

"We have a master on our hands then," the woman stated.

"What makes you say that?"

"Well," she walked out of the apartment and stared across the hallway at a different residence. The door was dark grey with black blotches, burnt. "This apartment was destroyed in the fire as well." She tilted her head, looking down the hall. "The one next door was not, and if it was the same fire that did all of this, then why is the hallway not burnt as well? And look!" She pointed at the supposed pile of a dead person on the floor. "The damage seems to radiate. It's like the fire's source began at that ash pile and spread outward." She poked her chin, shaking her head in confusion.

Zarek met the woman's questioning gaze. "Spontaneous combustion?" he offered, giving her his boyish grin.

"Doubtful," she muttered as the corner of her lip turned up. Something then caught her attention. A small teddy bear leaned against the doorway across from the couple. It had been charred, missing half of its face. She frowned, and Zarek turned his attention to the object.

"You want to know something else that's weird?" the man asked her.

"What?"

"Not a single child was killed." Ilayda tore away her gaze, and she looked at him with a sparking interest.

"So, the pyro knew whom he was killing and which apartments had children. Possibly a resident himself?"

"Not quite," the man said as he ran a hand through his hair, messing it into disorganized spikes. "Even though the children survived, the parents were killed in the fire. In fact, all the children were unharmed, not even a scratch on them."

Ilayda stared down the hall, overlooking the random burnt doors lining the walls. She had dealt with multiple fire cases, homicides, and even missing persons, but she had never seen anything like this. Her eyes fell onto something small lying on the floor halfway down the hall.

"Looks like we've got ourselves quite the case, Ilayda." Her colleague walked with her, his dress shoes thudding heavily across the wooden floors, which should have quickly burned in the fire.

Ilayda picked up the small item and turned it over in her hand. "Indeed, we do…" she whispered. The man looked over her shoulder to see what discovery she had made. In her hand was something that appeared to be a charred feather. Zarek raised an eyebrow, matching the woman's same expression. "A very peculiar case…."

A small child stood atop a twenty-story building, watching from afar the blazing erosion of the city. Flickers of orange and red reflected against her crystalline eyes. Her expression remained blank. Skyscrapers, cars, and lamp posts all submerged within a fiery wave. The people's screams stopped long ago, leaving only an eerie silence among the crackling hiss below. Not a thought process occurred within her until she felt the presence beside her.

As she twisted her head to the side, her blonde ponytail spiraled in the breeze, swirling about her ash-covered neck. The torn and dirty silken dress she wore blew toward the source of her new curiosity. Lavender flowered print matched the buckles of her white, now dusty, colored shoes. Her eyes remained unmoving as she tilted her head.

"Are you the one who caused all these fires?" She asked but received no response. "Of course you are. It's logical to come to that assumption." She spoke softly, her voice monotonous. "I cannot find my parents. I assume they are long lost in that fire down there." She gazed directly into the amber-colored orbs staring right back at her. "You don't talk much. I find it impolite, but that's okay; I think I understand."

A hand lifted, rising toward the little girl's chest. She smiled softly, watching a long finger point to the left side of her upper body where her dress had torn and she was exposed. The child either did not notice or did not care about her wardrobe malfunction.

"Will you burn me too?" she asked.

The response was a blast of light radiating from the finger toward her chest, shooting into her core where her heart should have been. Flame erupted within her, winding and coiling, creating something new. The light illuminated inside her, rays bouncing around her form as her clothing and hair blew in all directions, tangling. Then, she began to scorch in some places. The heat would have overwhelmed most humans, but the child remained unmoving. She merely watched, feeling a new life burning inside.

FEATHERS

A BLOOD-RED sun hung high in the sky, casting an orangish hue upon the pyramids of Tenochtitlan. Cries filled the air, half in worship and cheers, the other half in sorrow from the surrounding enslaved people who were to be offered as a sacrifice that night. Blood dripped down the stone steps, mixing with the dust. The wind churned, kicking up spiraling funnels along the edges of the pathway.

Guatemoc watched from the side of the stone slab where one of the maids lay. She mumbled to herself in prayer, confident that her sacrifice would provide enough to please the gods. Guatemoc would be next, and the small girl behind him would follow. It was the time of Hueytozoztli. The people worshipped multiple gods during this time, but Guatemoc focused on one precisely, begging the creator god to end such a visceral tradition. He was young but still never understood the logic behind the sacrificial offerings. He thought them to be cruel and disgusting. When he voiced his opinion to his parents, he was gladly offered to the priests for use during the next ritual. Guatemoc hated his parents. He also loathed those who occupied the temple's foot and danced and sang as they stabbed and cut themselves to offer their own blood during the ceremony.

Tiny sniffles came from behind him. The little girl was frightened, and he didn't blame her. He heard from the whispering slaves that the child's parents gave her away, not because they favored her but because they found her useless. She wasn't as pretty as her other sisters. Guatemoc stepped to the side, blocking the little girl's view. They remained inside the temple, awaiting their turn as a priest marked their bodies with paint. The elderly man, with his gaunt figure and sunken eyes, frightened the girl even further. The priest had the expression of a madman. He most likely partook in eating the sacrificial body parts in the past, if not to this day. Usually, the warriors fed on their captured human offerings, but this priest clearly thought himself powerful.

A flint knife rose into the air and quickly sunk into the maid, who lay on a slab in the staging area. She screamed, yet her words continued to spill out of her mouth as she worshipped the gods. The priest with the knife sliced into her, deep beneath her abdomen, up through her diaphragm. As she sputtered and gasped, her body twitched, and the priest promptly removed her heart with a sickening pop. The four others surrounding her babbled incoherently.

Guatemoc felt a tug on his hands. He quickly fought back and pulled away. The gaunt man wanted to take his feathers away. The boy collected them for months and planned to use them as an offering during his own sacrifice. The elderly man growled with distaste and shoved the boy into the open. The crowd cheered as the maid's body was tossed over the side of the pyramid, her corpse bouncing and cracking as it fell down the steps, blood splattering across the surface.

The boy paid the men no mind and covered the stained slab with the feathers he had brought. The leading priest noticed and called out to the crowd, waving his bloody knife through the air. He was pleased by the boy's additional offering. Guatemoc avoided their maddened gazes and climbed atop the stone slab, laying back on the bed of feathers. He only looked back once, giving the little girl a saddened expression. She didn't deserve this. She was far too young to understand what was going on. The haggard priest firmly held him down while the four others on either side started their frantic chants. Guatemoc didn't fight back; he felt no need to. He had a bigger plan, one that they would not expect. As the boy gazed at the sun, he silently prayed to the feathered serpent deity to end such activities.

Guatemoc barely made a sound as the knife plunged deep into his lower abdomen. He kept his focus on the sun, his mind on prayer. The wind suddenly picked up as the blade sliced through his torso. Thunder roared, and lightning cracked along the top of the temple. The priests and attendants cheered. The boy's sacrifice seemed to have reached the gods. Many were pleased.

A low growl sounded on the horizon, and the temple shook. A deep crevice spread along the pyramid's base, swallowing the dead bodies that had covered the end of the pathway. The leading priest continued slicing up the boy's chest and reached for his heart. The ground splintered further, and many of the enslaved people and members of the gathered crowd willfully jumped within. Lightning cracked the earth, and a monstrous call followed as the man removed Guatemoc's heart. The boy exhaled sharply, his body running cold.

His final vision was the great Quetzalcoatl rising before the pyramid, its lightning and slicing gales slaughtering those around him. Splatters of blood and matter caked the temple, and the priests fell to their knees in offering and mixed fear. The god spiraled around the men, devouring them whole. Quetzalcoatl was a creator god and hated the act of human sacrifice. The feathered serpent locked eyes with the boy, and Guatemoc died instantly, knowing his prayers had been answered.

DEAD LEAVES

I LEANED against a tree to take a break from my grueling chores, daydreaming as I waited for my love to return. I hadn't seen him in months, not one single trace. Our work separated us for extended periods each year. Occasionally, I would catch a hint of him in a cool breeze or an overturned rock. Whenever a whispering storm would slip over the ocean's waves, cooling the sands, I would see older couples holding hands, wearing their coats during a temperature those in other lands would consider warm. It made me smile, my heart pounding with each simple remembrance of him—sweaters, boots, mittens, warm drinks, the scent of cinnamon, and the approaching holidays.

I wiped a bead of sweat from my forehead. It seemed the last few weeks always grew hotter before my work ended. I tended to the gardens, ensuring the animals and insects had enough to eat and plenty of time to prepare for the oncoming cold. I walked by the riverbeds, talking to the fish and deer. Rain followed me as I journeyed across the lands. Every day, I kept myself busy. Many relied on me, and I relied on the distraction until I could vacate into my lover's arms. It was indeed cruel that our lives required isolation for so long, but it was an obligation we had both signed up for. Our jobs were our existence, the essence of our beings, and we wouldn't dare risk breaking the cycle. Too many lives depended on us.

I crossed the deserts, plains, and lakes and climbed into the mountains, tending to everything necessary. The further north I journeyed, the more I felt him close by. Sometimes, I slid onto the peaks, chancing a taste of the chilly air and wet snow. If I tarried too long, I could cause trouble. It was often his territory during my schedule's beginning and later months.

In the snowy peaks, I felt his touch. He could feel mine with the pine trees and yellow flowers next to the warm springs. And as our periods transitioned, we would trade places in the world, his talents painting the landscapes I had previously affected. Together, we would tango across the lands and over the oceans, our influence leaving traces of our fingerprints and voices, recognizable signatures that we could pick up as gifts to remind each other that we were still there and very much in love.

Something beautiful caught my eye as I walked along my usual path toward my original home. I approached the tree where we had first met, the one we had carved our love into. A burst of color tickled the edges of the foliage. The horizon blended from a hue of green to orange—like the color of my eyes looking into his. I felt a light crunch beneath my step, and my body shivered excitedly. Dead leaves coated the ground at the tree's base.

"Hello, Summer," his low, calm voice called out.

I circled the breadth of the tree trunk, locking my gaze with his, and giggled, twirling a browned leaf in my fingertips. He was finally here. We would be allowed to work in each other's presence for at least a while before I had to leave. I stepped on my tiptoes, the dead leaves crunching beneath my movement, and kissed his slightly chapped lips.

"Hello, Winter," I replied.

CHANGE

MELODY WAS your typical good Christian schoolgirl. She lived by the Bible and read it each night before bed. She attended all her classes on time, went to church on Sundays, and participated in the youth group and bible study each week. Melody ensured her uniform remained in peak condition and swapped out her stockings whenever they got a hole or a stain. She shined her shoes, bleached her shirts, and kept her skirt hemmed right above the knee, no longer and no shorter. She bathed every morning, blow-dried her hair, and curled it so that her dirty-blonde pigtails bounced just above her shoulders. She brushed her teeth for the full two minutes, flossed, and used mouthwash. Melody never wore makeup besides a bit of Chapstick during the winter to keep her lips in good condition. She worked out because her body was a temple, and she needed to care for it. She never tanned, had no tattoos, and refrained from drinking and smoking. She was the perfection the church liked to see. She was every bit the student she needed to be. Until the end of days came. And then she changed.

Melody stood upon a platform of marble. People cowered before the angels and the God that sat upon the golden throne—a blinding beacon of light with barely a shape or form. Still, the human mind understood who it was to be. Everyone's perception was slightly different than the others. Nervous beneath the ethereal stare, Melody awaited her turn for judgment. Fear settled within her belly; had she been good enough? Had she sacrificed enough? She kneeled before the throne, awaiting the decision of whether or not she would go to Heaven. Much to her surprise, a golden sword tapped her on the shoulder, granting her ultimate power.

Melody transformed, her body becoming a sight of perfection. Her mind's eye opened to the truths of the universe, and she finally understood everything—Heaven, Hell, time travel, alternate dimensions, and the reality of what mythological creatures actually were.

"You will be one of our soldiers. Do you accept your new fate?" one of the angels spoke, pulling her to the side as the Lord continued his judgment.

"I do," Melody confirmed.

"As judgment is passed, you shall guide souls to their chosen plane. Heaven or Hell, the decision is up to the Lord, but you will make sure those judged will follow through with their passage. You shall be granted proper ruling to take any who have influenced your life to their proper places. The Lord trusts you and your claims. The penalty of false accusation will cost you your soul. Do you accept this task?"

Melody quaked with anxiety as she felt a new power course through her veins. The energy bestowed upon her was immense, and she had an opportunity to prove herself to the God she had always trusted. "I accept. I will do my best to pass judgment properly. If I fail to do so correctly, you and the Lord shall punish me accordingly."

Too much power had been entrusted to her. Melody thought long and hard, watching the tears stream down the faces of those she had once loved. At least, she thought she had loved them. Looking back into her memories, she realized how many monsters she had allowed into her life. Family wasn't merely about blood. Her mother was trash and had harmed her psychologically in many ways. Her father, hiding behind his pious personality, was an abusive alcoholic. Though mentally strained by the lifestyle they both experienced, her sister was also a terrible human being. She lived off others, depending on them to pay for her drug habit, as she refused to find honest work. Lying and stealing weren't beneath Melody's sister. She was a drain on the system and felt entitled to a free ride to party and use everyone she could, doing nothing but dampening the mental sanity of those around her. And Melody's friends, her closest friends, were just as bad. They bullied her throughout her life. She had been made fun of for her looks, health issues, and love for certain people. Her friends had sleepovers and talked behind her back. They would purposefully find out whom she liked and promptly dated the individual simply to break her heart. And as Melody aged, her friends twisted further into a muck of jealousy and hate.

Melody spent her life supporting and loving those around her, accepting the abuse because she thought that was what God would want her to do. She thought that was the right thing to do. She remembered her college years and how boys lied to and used her and remembered the friends who slept with her lovers because they found it amusing to make her cry. She thought of the men who lured her in to break her heart and use her for sex. Melody hated herself. Her parents wanted her to save herself for marriage, but the men she loved were too good at manipulating her into giving her body away.

Melody narrowed her eyes, gazing at the line covering the horizon. Millions made it to the area, yet a highlight of each person she had ever known filtered into her sight. She recognized everyone, accessing their every memory and thought, weighing their words and actions between good and evil, and deciding on the afterlife she felt they deserved.

"Are you ready?" the angel asked her.

"I am," she answered with vigor.

The angel handed her a staff imbued with the inherent ethereal properties she would need. "Then go. We trust you with your decisions."

Feeling a bit more excited than she thought she would ever be, Melody confronted those who had hurt her. She levitated above the crowd, soaring toward her targets. Family members, left and right, were tossed into the deep, crackling crevice stretching beside them. Pious liars. Adulterers, abusers, rapists, scum. She hated most of the lot, her rage consuming her. However, her humility returned with each person she encountered who had treated her well and begged for her forgiveness. Many had pled, but she knew who genuinely meant it, and those few received access to the heavens.

"Melody?" one man questioned out of the masses. She turned and came face to face with one of her pastors. The man hadn't disappeared upon the rapture, which meant something was amiss.

"Pastor Davis," Melody acknowledged the man.

"Is that really you?" he asked.

"It is."

"My…how you have changed."

The words struck her hard. "What do you mean?"

"You were once so innocent, so eager to listen and learn. And now…you seem like an angel of death. You look as if you enjoy tossing the others into the pit of Hell." The man gazed upon her with watering eyes.

Melody cowered beneath the man's gaze for only a moment. Had she turned into a monster? Perhaps she was unkind to everyone. Maybe they all deserved forgiveness. She began to question herself.

"You were so young when you attended my church. Now, look at you. Full-grown and full of a fire that I have never seen." The man eyed her up and down, clearly enjoying the new form of perfection her image took. Melody scowled.

In an instant, many suppressed memories flooded her senses. She was young when the pastor would ask her to stay late after bible study. He liked her innocent appearance and how her pigtails flowed to her shoulders. He mentioned it weekly. And he made sure to comment on her pristine uniform. At first, Melody liked the compliments and attention, but she had forgotten how he would touch her somewhere along the line. It started harmlessly enough, him touching her shoulders and hands. Then, he would tickle her thighs and stomach. He had made her feel special, had reminded her that she was God's gift and that he had to make sure no man took her womanhood before he did. He was God's vessel, and God needed to claim her before any man did.

Melody dropped her staff, gazing at the man in fear. Pastor or not, he was a liar and a cheat, and now that she had gained ultimate knowledge and awareness, she knew all of his deceit. With a scream, she grabbed her weapon, aiming it at the man who had tried to look over her with a lustful gaze, her memories scarring her brain.

"You are condemned to Hell!" she shrieked.

The man cowered in fear. Did he actually believe he could hide behind the church and still receive forgiveness? People like Melody owned the crowd. And now, it all became clear. She was to pass judgment upon those who hid behind the clarity and love of God's mission. This man was not who he said he was. He was a tainted individual, a disgusting creature that preyed upon the weak, misguided, and fearful.

Melody soared toward him, and the earth shattered into pieces around her. She flew high into the air, gazing into the older man's eyes, seeing all the victims he had hurt. "There is no forgiveness for you. Saying, 'I believe,' is not enough. You are weak and disgusting."

Without another thought, she tossed the man into the river of fire as the others screamed and ran. The man was correct. She had changed. Melody was no longer a frightened girl. She knew the truth, could see it clearly, and her job was to rid the earth and the heavens of those who hid behind the guise of innocence and love.

CANDY WRAPPER

SWEAT DRIPPED down my back, reminding me how uncomfortable my long-sleeve dress was. The sun beat down on us despite the cloudy forecast with a chance of rain. I shuffled in my heels, trying not to sink back into the soft soil behind me. I had hoped it would be cool like the weather had been the following week. Of course, now it would be uncharacteristically hot for the autumn season. Still, better than a torrential downpour, I suppose.

On top of all the sweat, my makeup smeared beneath my salty tears, making things worse. I just wanted to go home, shower, and cry with a tub of ice cream. But the irony that the day was sunny and hot wasn't lost on me. It was his favorite kind of weather, and what I wore was one of his favorite outfits. According to him, it hugged all the right curves—it was sexy yet modest and professional. The outfit made me feel worse, as he couldn't see me in it. Why did I bother to hold on to such sentimental things? It's not like he would be able to tell. It's not like he would ever compliment these things ever again.

I sniffed, half choking on a sob. A few people looked toward me, making everything even more awkward. I hated it. I hated being in churches, and I hated cemeteries. I hated the color of his casket, and I hated the ill-fitting dress coat his mother chose for him to wear. He disliked brown. He didn't like dressing up. He loathed having his hair parted sideways. Where were his torn jeans, ball cap, and silly t-shirt? And those shoes. Did she buy them at a thrift store just for the occasion? They didn't fit right, and I don't think I had ever seen him wear a pair like that. I hated everything about this day. That was not my funny, loud-mouthed Andrew. No, this corpse before me was nothing but a ghostly image, a copy of the man I loved.

I couldn't look any longer. Nothing felt right, and I still couldn't believe he was gone. As I peered over those gathered for the burial service, I expected him to be among the others, by his friends, his brothers. Still, I didn't see his green eyes or crooked smile, and I couldn't hear his loud laughter. This man was my everything—my life, my joy. He was the only one ever to make me genuinely happy. He'd saved me just as I thought my life was over. And now, he was gone, taken by a drunk driver the night of our anniversary.

"I shouldn't have made him rush home. I shouldn't have made a big deal about our dinner plans," I whispered into my tissue, blowing my nose. Someone rubbed my shoulder, assuring me that it was not my fault.

In the blink of an eye, my revival had ended. The one who had breathed life into me no longer existed, and he took my soul with him. What was I going to do? Our home was empty without him. Quiet. Dark. Cold. What was I to do about the dog? He was already depressed that his father had never come home. And our cat, well, she had been howling every morning at the door as she waited for him. They both already covered his side of the bed with their fur. The thought made my heart sink into my stomach, and I wailed, hyperventilating.

Before I knew it, I realized I was one of the few who lingered in the cemetery. The service had long since ended, yet I remained by the hole in the ground, gaping at the wooden box that enclosed him. The workers had arrived to take down the tent and cover the plot. They chatted quietly, a casual conversation during their regular job. Still, one set of eyes would peer at me now and then with an expression of pity. I sighed. I wanted to go home so badly, but at the same time, I didn't want to leave him. This was it. This was my last time ever to be this close to him.

"Andrew," I said between a shaking sob. "Halloween is tomorrow. I…I brought you your favorite candy."

A cool breeze hugged my form, and I shivered. The clouds churned, blocking the sunlight. Finally, the forecasted rain had arrived. Light taps of raindrops sounded above me against the cover of the tent. I knew now that I had better leave soon as the workers still had much to do, and I had probably ruined their plans to finish work quickly before the storm arrived. I reached into my pocket and retrieved a pair of black and orange wrapped candies. Andrew always loved the "old man" sweets. The tacky, chalky, peanut butter kind was his absolute favorite. We always bought a bag to hand out to the kids, and by the end of the night, he had his own stash, as nobody ever chose to take that kind over the candy bars and bubblegum. The thought made me cry harder. What in the hell would I do with all that candy now?

I crouched, gently dropping the orange-wrapped taffy onto his casket. I kept the black one for myself. I undid it and shoved the waxy treat into my mouth. Crying while eating was always awful, but this chewy, bland mess was the worst thing I had ever tasted. Everything was wrong. All of this was wrong. It took four attempts to swallow the treat. I silently had hoped I would choke on it. After a loud eruption of thunder, I shook and sighed heavily.

"Well, I better get going. I'll visit you as much as possible. I'll bring you candy every time. I have enough to last me a lifetime, it seems." I tried to laugh, but only more tears came. "I love you, baby. I love you so much. Please, come back to me."

I forced myself to turn away, shuffling in my wobbly heels as I approached the car. The rain had picked up as I climbed into the vehicle. As I slammed the door shut, everything fell into a deep silence. I couldn't even hear the thunder or pounding rain as I screamed, feeling my insides shatter into a thousand pieces. I felt like my life was over. How was I going to survive without him? Who was going to hug me during my hard times? Make me laugh when others could not? How was anything ever going to be okay again?

I don't know how I got home. I only remember it was nearly dark when I arrived at my destination. I walked so slowly to the house that my clothes were thoroughly soaked. I forced myself through the home's entry, kicked off my shoes, and shuffled to the back bedroom. Neither the dog nor cat greeted me, which was odd, but it seemed apparent why they wouldn't. I remained numb. I could no longer cry, but every breath was a quaking shudder that left a stabbing pain in my chest. It didn't matter that my clothes were wet. To lie in bed was all that I wanted, curled up on my side while holding his pillow.

I entered the room and noticed my furry children had occupied his side, just as they had when I left for the funeral that morning. As I was about to start another tirade of cries, to tell them that their daddy was gone, something caught my eye, making me stop dead in my tracks.

There, on Andrew's pillow, lay something orange-colored. I approached his side of the bed, my mouth hanging open as I blankly stared at the object. It was wrinkled and wet. Slowly, I lifted the waxy paper. As I looked over it, the scent of stale peanut butter wafted through the room. And, just like that, I cried once again, clutching the item against my chest. I dropped to the carpet, feeling the sun's heat as it shimmered between a gap in the clouds through the window. It warmed me, and I laughed. No, I was wrong. Everything was going to be okay. I would be all right, and the cat and dog would be fine. We would somehow survive and get through this one day at a time. Within a minute, I already felt better. And it was all because of a wet candy wrapper.

CALM

THEY SAY animals can sense fear. They can smell it on you like you had
bathed in it. When *they* came, they sensed it in everyone, and the hunt became
easy. The creatures don't have ordinary senses as we know them. They don't
need eyes, don't need ears. All they require is their keen sense of smell. And
even then, it isn't like how we comprehend the usage of smell through our
noses. No, these things can feel our emotions, taste them, and cleanse
themselves with them.

To make matters worse, *they* aren't your typical material beings. These
things can pop in and out of our realm instantaneously. They can sense us
from beyond the veil, unknowingly tracking us behind the scenes.

I was one of the lucky ones, I suppose. I didn't have a wife or children. I
never cared much for those things. Having a family was nothing more than
a hassle, a blockade to everything I wanted and desired most. So, when people
were dropping like flies left and right, the essence of their very being ripped
from their bodies—sucked dry—I didn't lose too many individuals that I
otherwise would have missed. I guess that's one of the perks of being a
Sociopath. Or was I a psychopath? Maybe I'm a mixture of both, but why
should that be a bad thing? It's what kept me alive all this time. I've fought

several wars and killed more than just a man or two outside the battlefield. Some labeled me as a bad guy, but it wasn't like I was raping and killing women and children. No, sometimes I would cross paths with the right asshole, and I did the world a favor by taking them out.

Having a mental illness often comes with a stigma. I understand all the mumbo jumbo that my therapists shoved down my throat. At least I had the decency to separate myself from the rest of society and protect everyone else from me. I never gathered much pleasure from manipulating and twisting people's lives around mine. However, when it came to my life and career, I'd do whatever it takes to be on top. So, when I heard about these strange creatures—if you can even call them that—I finally had a new challenge to overcome.

I hooked up a hose to the cylindrical plastic container in the corner of my bedroom. It was about my height and twice as wide. I turned on a radio beside the wonky device I had created, allowing the static to flow through the room. A light bulb inside the container strobed with the sound of the radio hiss while a seismic device at the side collected vibration frequencies. I reached for the small cage on my nightstand, retrieved the mouse inside, and placed it within the container. It immediately swirled in circles, trying to find a way to escape.

"Sorry, lil guy, but your sacrifice is needed," I muttered as I sucked on my cigarette.

I wasn't just a grunt. I operated in the science division of the military long before I decided I preferred killing people. I worked on some of the government's most top-secret projects. "Mr. Black Book" is what they called me when I worked in the field. It didn't begin with me, however. My father and grandfather both worked on the Montauk Project. My grandfather started his work early during the Philadelphia experiments and was transferred to Montauk once they pulled the plug after the Eldridge disaster.

And no, funding was never cut from the program. The project names and studies merely changed facilities over the years, one disaster after another. When I left the labs to play soldier, the government continued operations on interdimensional travel. I had lost interest long ago. I'd seen enough shit to know that it was only a matter of time before we doomed ourselves by either imploding our universe or bringing something here that didn't belong. Obviously, the latter happened.

I watched the mouse scurry about with little sympathy. I couldn't feel much for the thing, perhaps only a smidgeon more than I did for most humans. My mental state might have directly resulted from all of the mind-bending experiments my lineage took part in. Those who survived the exposure to interdimensional travel either met their death, a slew of physical abnormalities, or insanity. My family's emotional deficiencies weren't deemed the healthiest, but as I watched the mouse squeak with fear as I tapped the glass, I knew that we had evolved to become survivors.

"Yes, yes. Be afraid, lil mouse, just a bit longer."

The radio static grew loud; the pulses became even-paced. The light strobe matched the beat, and the mouse hopped around. *It* was coming, falling right into my trap. With a jump and a squeak, the mouse pressed against the bottom of the container, fighting back an invisible force. It trembled, and a gust of air moved its fur as something sucked out its life force. I reached for the power button of the radio and silenced it. The light clicked on, and slowly, the thing apparated inside the container. It wasn't solid in form yet held a strange ghostly structure—not quite human, but not an animal.

"I see you," I tapped on the glass. The thing soared about, its limbs swirling against the plastic covering. "Meh, not so scary, are you?" I blew smoke against the container where I assumed its face was.

I stretched, cracked my spine, and dropped onto the bed in the opposite corner. With a sigh, I laid back. It was time for a nap.

"Get used to it. That's your new home. Either you figure things out and become friendly, or you'll starve…like all the others." I put out my cigarette and relaxed against my pillow.

One after another, I hunted them. They had to feed hourly, or they would starve to death by the next day, turning into a strange mist that I collected via a vacuum. After gathering enough specimens, I planned to go to the underground tunnels to find the secret labs the government had supposedly shut down. I hoped to learn more about these creatures, where they came from, and whether or not they had any intelligence. By the end of the month, I figured I would collect enough. Besides, it was easy to catch one of the things. All I had to do was remain calm.

BLIND DATE

CAROLYN ENTERED the restaurant approximately five minutes late for her date. She had waited at her car, eyeing each man who arrived alone, judging them appropriately by the photos and descriptions sent to her. When she saw one man who matched the picture, she waited a few minutes longer, gathering her nerves before entering the classy restaurant.

"John?" she nervously asked as she approached a table with her hands gathered against her chest.

"Ah! Yes! Carolyn?" The man in the blue dress shirt and black slacks rose and lightly shook her hand.

"Yes! I'm so sorry I'm late." She lightly grasped his fingers and sat across from him, smoothing the wrinkles from her red dress. It hugged her curves but flowed at her waist—pretty, sexy, yet modest enough. She wore light makeup, had painted her nails red, and had curled her blonde shoulder-length hair. She had a classic beauty.

"Oh, only a few minutes! No problem at all! If it had been an hour though…." he laughed as he sat down again. The man had dark hair and matching eyes.

"I certainly hope that hasn't happened before."

The man sipped his water, giving a smug smile as he chuckled. "Perhaps once."

Carolyn laughed. She leaned forward in her seat with her hands folded in her lap. "I appreciate your honesty. And I shouldn't laugh, as I may have had the same thing happen to me before."

"So, we already have something in common!" The man smiled. "Wine?" he asked as he carefully poured a glass from a bottle he had already ordered.

Carolyn's eyes widened. "Oh my! Look at that! I can't refuse."

They shared a drink, lightly clinking their glasses together. "Well, to first dates and to those who are merely *fashionably* late," John said with a wink.

Carolyn giggled and sipped from the glass. "I like this red wine. Not too dry, not too sweet."

"Pairs well with meat and Italian dishes."

"Italian is my favorite."

The two ordered their meals, sharing the typical conversation many had during a first date. But as Carolyn ate her lasagna and John enjoyed his steak, the subject matter had somewhat dulled. Carolyn cleared her throat, wiping her red lips with a cloth napkin.

"Tell me, John, what are some of your hobbies?" she leaned forward. "Don't be shy. Tell me something interesting. Something that you usually don't tell anyone else."

"Well," John started, looking upward into the lights, "…it sounds weird, but I'm interested in reading."

"Why is that weird?"

"Well, I enjoy murder mysteries. I like solving puzzles and am intrigued by the psychology of it all."

Carolyn grinned. "Interesting!" She propped forward again, her eyes lighting up. "John, I work for the paper, and some of my favorite articles cover murder and strange mysteries. I mean, I feel sorrow for those involved, but I am also intrigued by such events. How funny."

John smirked as he tasted his wine. "I wouldn't have guessed you to be interested in such things."

Carolyn bobbed her head. "Oh, yes! I love true crime shows. Those television specials about missing people or unsolved crimes fascinate me."

"Have you seen the series on the New Hampshire killer?" John asked.

Carolyn's face dropped for only a second before she smirked again. "Of course, I have. Who hasn't?"

"That man…the killer. What do you think goes through his mind? Why does he choose his victims? It sometimes seems logical and other times…so erratic," John whispered.

Carolyn peered side to side, whispering as well. "You know what I really think?"

John gave her an expression that told her he was listening.

"I think it's two killers."

The man's mouth dropped open. "Really?" he asked as he sat back.

"Yeah. The motives seem entirely different in each case. Some have identical profiles and identities. Others, well, they seem like the opposite."

John chewed on his lip, sipping his wine. Suddenly, the night had become increasingly fascinating. "I haven't heard of that theory. Now that you mention it, perhaps that is possible."

The two gossiped and shared their favorite crime and murder stories, piecing together evidence and theories. John had only parted once to relieve himself as Carolyn ordered a second bottle. They drank more and chatted for hours. As the night came to a close, John noticed the servers cleaning the tables and vacuuming.

"Oh, dear. I believe we've closed down the place," he said with a laugh.

Carolyn looked around and nodded. "It seems we have."

They had long since closed their tab and paid their bill. John stood, retrieving his jacket. Carolyn did the same, and he led her outdoors. Snow lined the streets.

"Well, Carolyn, I must say that it has been quite a long while since I've enjoyed the company of another. I hate that the time has gone by so quickly."

"I enjoyed it as well. Thank you so very much for the wonderful dinner."

John nodded, eyeing the snow-covered streets. He prepared to ask Carolyn if she needed a ride in such weather, but she beat him to the punch.

"Say, John," Carolyn faced him. "Would you like…to maybe come back to my place? I have a couple of bottles of wine I've been saving, and there is a new show we could stream." She grinned. "One involving a treacherous tale of murder."

John laughed.

"That sounded incredibly creepy, didn't it?" Carolyn joined in his chuckling.

"My dear, I would love to," he replied with a glimmer in his eye. He pulled out his keys, but Carolyn took his hand.

"My car is right here. No sense in both of us driving in this weather." Carolyn chewed on her lower lip.

"Oh?" John looked at her with a shocked expression. "Oh, indeed. I, uh," he stammered a bit.

"Don't worry. I'm a mature woman. We can merely drink and enjoy each other's company. In the morning, I will take you to your car. It's coming down hard right now, and we both had much to drink."

"But are you okay to drive, missy?"

Carolyn laughed. "I only had two glasses, sir."

John blushed. "Had…had I drunk that much? I apologize."

"No worries. There's plenty more back at my place. If things progress further, I have a comfy couch and a comfier bed." Carolyn tugged him toward her little red car. John commented on how nice it was and slipped into the passenger seat.

"You know…" he spoke as the woman drove. His eyes grew heavy as the heat and defroster warmed him. "I honestly didn't expect this turn of events. Usually, my dates don't go so well."

"Well, maybe I'm not like many girls out here," Carolyn said, gazing at the sleepy man. She smiled. "Getting tired?"

John's demeanor changed a bit. "Yeah…I am…unnaturally tired. What the hell?"

Carolyn laughed and then yawned. As she drove, the snow in the headlights swirled. Drowsiness overtook her, and her head bobbed. Was there something wrong with the wine they drank?

She eyed the man, judging him. "Did…did you fucking drug me?" she asked.

"Did you fucking drug me?" he retorted.

Carolyn's head dipped, and she lost consciousness as the car eddied across the icy road, colliding with a tree. She woke up in a hospital bed the next day, strapped to an IV. She looked around the pallid room, trying to regain focus and memory of what had happened. Her thumb pressed against the call button, and a nurse hurried into her room and checked on her.

"What…what happened?" Carolyn asked.

"Oh, miss! You are so lucky! You were in a car wreck late last night," the nurse spoke quietly yet firmly.

Memories from the date flooded her mind. "J-John?"

"John? You mean that man you were with?" the nurse solemnly asked.

Carolyn nodded.

"Well, he's in jail, miss. It seems the car wreck was a bit of luck for you."

"Luck?"

"Well…you see, it appears that John is one of the suspects in the New Hampshire murders. His fingerprints match some of those found at the scene of one of the previous killings. I'm so glad you're all right, miss. Things could have ended up much worse."

Carolyn covered her face, sobbing.

"Let me get you some medicine and a glass of water really quick," the nurse rushed out of the room.

After a moment of waiting, Carolyn lowered her hands, laughing. "Oh, that idiot."

She leaned back with a sigh, her tired gaze drifting to the window. Snow continued to fall outside. A small smile crossed her face. Her plans for the past evening were ruined, but everything ended up working out in her favor. John was careless. He got in the way of her work and was nothing more than a copycat killer. His crimes were sloppy, and the mere fact that he had been confused with the New Hampshire killer annoyed her. She had built up a tolerance to Benzodiazepines over the years. However, the strength that John used was way over the top. Most likely, many of his victims OD'd on the drugs before he could carve into them. Carolyn sighed with relief. She planned to kill him. But with John captured and blamed for all the New Hampshire killings, it worked out better for her. Now, nobody would have any reason to suspect her.

"Try to take my glory, and I'll take your life," Carolyn muttered.

The nurse entered the room with a glass of water and a pill. The injured woman gratefully took the medication and relaxed into her bed, enjoying the view of the swirling white flakes. Though she loved the snow, she couldn't help but wonder about the weather in Florida.

ANGEL

THUMPING MUSIC, the scent of booze, loud chatter, and the grazing of shoulders as I passed through the crowd made me stumble more than I would have if I were in an empty hallway and not a whole bottle in. I definitely should not have had that last drink. Or two. I had long since forgotten how many I had downed. The girl I met kept buying me drinks, and I could not refuse. Besides, how often was it a girl bought a guy a drink? You bet your ass I was going to take advantage of the situation.

I tripped over someone's foot, spilling half my drink upon myself and another woman. She screamed at me, but I kept on moving forward. The caterwauling bleached blonde should know better than to wear her Pradaesque dress to a filthy club such as this. Spilled alcohol and patrons vomiting were a nightly ordeal. Who the hell wore stilettos to a club anyway? I never understood that—girls sauntering around in such absurd clothing while trying to dance to a fast-paced electronic pulse was laughable. She should have been at a Beyoncé concert, not stamping her feet like an angry cow while holding a cheap beer.

"Now, now, don't be judgmental," I mumbled to myself as I neared the bathrooms. It's not like I was a quality individual with my backward cap, torn jeans, and stained High Tops. I wasn't exactly a 'catch' or much of a 'winner' with my greasy hair, drug addiction, and a job at the local fast-food taco chain. Still, I at least knew better to drink the rum and cokes than ever to order the watered-down canned piss the bar served.

"I'm…somewhat classy," I chuckled, shouldering the wall to maintain balance. "Where the hell did she go?"

I had lost sight of the girl who had been buying me drinks. She had passed me the last one, whispered something about getting naughty in a quiet, dark place, and then disappeared. I was possibly a bit too intoxicated, but I wouldn't let that stop me.

She had a gothic nuance to her clubwear with her long, dark hair that curled over her shoulders, thick eyeliner, glimmering makeup, and glossy maroon lips. It was a style I usually overlooked, but something about how it accentuated her curves caught my attention. What was her name? Angel. That's right. She looked like one, smelled like heaven, and moved with a grace that only I could assume an angel could. However, she reeked of seduction, and I was excited just at the sight of her licking her lips.

"Hurry along, slow-poke," her ethereal voice echoed in my mind. I was close.

I stumbled toward the women's restroom, prepared for a female assault followed by a myriad of squawking protests. I had done many inappropriate things in the men's bathroom but never in the women's. I wondered whether it would be cleaner than the men's facility's stalls. I reached forward to open the door when another to my right flew open. My angel appeared in the threshold, her painted finger urging me to follow. A cool breeze met my face, and I chased after her into the dark alleyway behind the club.

"You're a playful one," I muttered, quickening my pace to follow her while she trotted behind a dumpster.

"Playful and dirty," I sighed. Perhaps Angel had an apartment close by that we could walk to. The dumpsters reeked of piss and rotten junk. Having the chance of whiskey-dick was going to be problematic enough without the issue of having to hold my breath from the rancid smell surrounding us. "Damn, it smells like something died out here." I covered my nose.

I passed by the first dumpster. The woman wasn't there. I pressed further, passing a second and then a third.

"Over here," her whisper echoed behind me.

Her taunting voice caused me to pause, and I finally noticed a hole that dug into the side of one of the neighboring buildings, leading into a crawl space. I crouched, eyeing the darkness within.

"You want me to go in there?" I asked. "No way." My curiosity got the better of me. It must not have been so bad if she was down there. I didn't want to be considered a pussy, so I leaned forward, peering further inside. "So, is this your secret place?"

"I have many secrets." Her voice came from behind me once again. I looked over my shoulder, catching her smoldering gaze. I could have sworn her voice came from the hole only moments before. How had I bypassed her without noticing? I must have been more drunk than I thought.

"Oh, yeah?" I smirked.

A low growl resonated from the darkness beside me, gaining my attention. I looked within the hole, coming face-to-face with a black silhouette and eyes that glowed with a fiery hue. I could barely scream before an invisible hand tugged me within. I fell, feeling the claws of a hundred hands ripping at my clothing and flesh. Further, I plummeted into the darkness, far more than should have been possible, my sight locked on the woman who stood outside the hole, whose figure faded with the distance. Her eyes showed no fear, no remorse. And before my vision faded to darkness, I saw her smile. The smile of an angel. My dark angel.

WISH

EVERY DAY, I spend time with my best friend whenever he comes home from school. It is my favorite time of day. I hold my friend in the highest regard and think he's the most outstanding and kindest person that exists. My friend, Caleb, always makes sure to spend time with me. We share snacks while he works on his homework, things I never understand. I wish I could read, but I've been told that I am dumb, which is probably why I'm not allowed to go to school despite wanting to do so very badly. But Caleb thinks I'm smart, and the only thing that matters is that we go to the park to play after homework. I love watching him swing. He can get higher than anyone else. Sometimes, I get nervous when he swings too high, but he surprises me by jumping out of the swing at full height and landing perfectly without hurting himself. I have no idea how he does that. It is impressive.

It was a typical day when I met Caleb at his front door, as always. However, he looked sad, and I couldn't help but worry about him. Any time Caleb came home feeling sad, that usually meant bad news. Perhaps he had failed a test; maybe the teachers were concerned about something and wanted his parents to meet with them. Either way, it was never good news.

Caleb passed by me, opening the door with his head hung low. He sulked as he walked toward his bedroom. I followed as usual, but his father called out to him. Caleb shrunk, cowering in a way that made me feel out of place.

"Caleb! Have you done your chores?" his father hollered. The man always made me anxious.

"I just got home," Caleb responded.

"It's 4:30! What took you so long to get home? Were you playing with that slut again?" His father pounded through the house, his footsteps growing louder as he approached the bedroom.

"No. I mean, she's not a slut, dad. She lives a block away. We walked home with our friends. We were all talking, and I lost track of time."

"That doesn't matter! You know you are supposed to be home no later than four!"

"Dad. We live over a mile away from school."

"I don't care how far we live from the school! I lived much further when I was your age, had to walk home in the rain and snow, and still was home when my father wanted me to!" Caleb's father shouted.

I curled up, hiding the best I could behind Caleb's door. I hated his father. He was mean and abusive and treated everyone in the house with disrespect. Every night, it seemed to be the same thing. Caleb would arrive home as soon as possible and do all his homework before dinner, but nothing would matter. His dad would smack him, yell at him, and blame him for their family's problems. Despite what I wanted, I couldn't help. I was scared. My friend was alone in the fight. With her black eyes and bruised arms, his mother would hide in the corner of the room. I felt helpless.

One night, as Caleb's father tossed him into the hallway, I yelled as loud as possible, pulled on the man's sleeve, and did all I could to get him to leave my friend alone. Caleb never did anything wrong. He tried his best in school and hurried through his chores each day. He played with me, talked to his mom every night, and made sure she was safe and happy. I admired Caleb. He was more of a man than his father ever was.

"I told you to do the dishes! Why haven't you done them yet?" his father shouted as he punched Caleb.

"I was going to…but you told me to finish my homework," Caleb said between each hit.

"It's after dinner; you do homework before!"

I shouted. I tried my best, but his father swatted me across the nose, and I fell against the wall. Oh, it hurt so much. Who did this man think he was? Not a father or a protector, I knew that much. With a cry, I ran outside. It was dark now, the full moon rising high into the sky.

I looked upon the moon and stars, the crisp winter air blowing my hair around me. I could hear my friend as his father pummeled him in the hallway of his home. I was desperate. I needed my friend to be safe.

Please, moon. Grant me the strength I need to save my friend. I wish him nothing but safety and happiness.

As I stared at the shimmering moon, I felt a power rise deep within my belly. The sound of a thousand howls rang in my ears, and I whimpered, feeling euphoric and afraid as my body transformed into something more sinister. Long claws stretched from my fingertips. My hair grew wildly and covered my body, my tail flipping in the wind. My ears elongated, and my snout grew larger with piercing teeth. My claws dug deep into the earth as I let out a howl most feral. The sound echoed within the darkness of the night, and I ran back indoors, the weight of my thick, muscular body cracking the doorframe, my paws tearing at the linoleum floor.

I ripped across the kitchen, howling at the man who beat my friend in the hallway, my mouth opening to let out a ferocious howl.

"What the hell are you?" the grown man shouted as I cornered him and placed my body between his and my friend's.

I glared, giving him my meanest stare.

"Get outta here! This is none of your business!" the man bellowed.

I couldn't take it anymore. Caleb's father tried punching and kicking at me, but I dodged his blows. The next time his fist swung at me, I latched on with my enormous jaws, growling as I viciously tightened my bite around his fist. He screamed, and I only sank my teeth further, tearing at his flesh. Once I ripped his right arm to shreds, I snatched his left, doing the same damage. The man dropped to the floor as a blind rage took over me with the taste of his blood. I looked at Caleb, who was bruised and scraped up. I noticed his mother cowering in the kitchen, crying and covering her black eye. I couldn't deal with it anymore. I loved these people. They were my friends, and they took care of me and fed me. Caleb's father or not, I wouldn't let him abuse them anymore.

I latched onto the man's throat, my jaws tightening. I tasted nothing but blood. Though it wasn't necessarily a flavor I enjoyed, I felt that it satisfied the moon, which I had wished upon, so I sank my teeth further into the man's neck, growling and thrashing him about until Caleb's voice finally reached me.

"No! No more! No more, Lucky! He's dead! Let him go!"

I quickly released the man from my vicious hold, eyeing the boy who tried his best to calm me. I felt his fingers dig into my fur, petting me.

"It's okay, Lucky. Just stop. Please."

I sat back, panting, my tail wagging back and forth. Caleb scratched me behind the ears as my fur settled against my body. His mother quickly approached us with a wet rag, wiping my face. She was always gentle with me. Caleb and his mother whispered to one another for quite a while, eyeing me now and then. Perhaps I had gone a bit overboard. However, I followed them outside to the backyard, where they began digging. I joined them. Digging was always fun. By daybreak, we had created an enormous hole.

Caleb and his mother tossed the terrible man into the pit. I didn't see him move or speak, but blood covered him.

"It's okay, Lucky. We know you were trying to protect us. But if we called the police, they would have you put down. We want to keep you forever. You are a good dog. You protected us." Caleb pet me between the ears.

Good dog. That's all I wanted to hear. And from then on, I knew I would forever protect them because that is what good dogs do.

LOST KEY

HIDE-AND-SEEK used to be one of my favorite games. My little
brother and I played it all the time. We were good at cheating, too, hiding in
one location until the seeker would pass by and then running to hide in a spot
they had already checked. We would waste hours together playing. It got to
the point where our parents had allowed us to stay home alone simply
because they knew we were good at entertaining ourselves. However, that all
changed two years ago…when my brother disappeared.

Mom and Dad had left us at home while they went into town for dinner
and a movie. It was a relatively new house for us; we had only lived there a
few months. Still, Joey and I had played enough hide-and-seek to know every
nook and cranny of the place. That's why it was so strange when he
disappeared that particular evening. It was my turn to be the seeker. I counted
to thirty while he hid, and it was an excruciating thirty seconds. I had gotten
exceptionally good at predicting his hiding places, and he had recently
become annoyed that I found him so quickly. So, that night, he bragged about
having the perfect hiding place. I didn't believe him. I had scoured the home

in my free time for the best hiding places. There was nowhere I didn't know about. At least not the ones we had access to.

I searched the entire house that night. Joey was nowhere to be found. It had grown extra dark from the approaching storm, but we continued to play with the lights out, one of our favorite things to do, as it added to the suspense. Eventually, after checking every dark shadow in the house, I turned on the lights, calling out for him. I stood in the center of the home, listening. I heard no floorboards creak, no giggling, no breathing, absolutely nothing outside of the wind and the rain. Joey knew better than to go outside for hide-and-seek. We either played only in the house or only outdoors. And with our parents gone, we were restricted to staying indoors, especially in the evening and definitely during a storm. Still, something bothered me. With all my heart, I knew my brother was no longer in the house. The cheerful vibe of the home had turned into a strange feeling of emptiness. A shiver of fear crept over me, and I rushed outside.

I worried that he had gone out into the woods behind the house. He had bragged about having a new hiding spot. Guilt washed over me as I searched outside in the violent wind and rain. Maybe I should have let him win the game more often. I checked behind every tree in our yard, under the cars, the garage, shed, and dumpsters. There was still no sign of Joey. The last place I examined was the old tornado shelter that burrowed deep underground. Dad had told us to stay away from the old cellar many times, that it wasn't safe. Joey knew this. Besides, according to the previous owners, it remained locked as the key went missing over twenty years ago. Still, I tried the door anyway. I tugged with all my might, yet the old entry didn't budge. The wind was cruel, breaking a few tree branches above me. I moved back as they crashed down onto the shelter door. I was scared, cold, and wet. There was no way Joey was out there. I had only put myself at risk by being out in the violent storm, so I went back inside, where I continued my search and yelled for my brother until my parents came home.

Together, we searched all over once again. We never found Joey. The police searched the woods. We hung posters throughout the town. There had been no reports of any other missing children, and the crime rates were low in the area. The possibility of someone abducting Joey was slim, though we never set that prospect aside. After six months, we had started to lose hope. By a year, Mom and Dad had grown cold and distant. I blamed myself, of course. I was the older sibling. How I lost my little brother was a mystery. Rumors had spread throughout the school that I was responsible for his disappearance, that I had killed him and hid his body. Eventually, I stopped going to class. Therapy didn't work. And my parents decided it was time to move away and start over. The hardest part of that decision was the fact that my parents had finally given up. Joey was gone. Most likely, we weren't ever going to see him again.

And it was around that time that the dreams got worse. Now and then, Joey would appear during my sleep. Usually, we played hide-and-seek or ate at our favorite burger joint in town, but the recent dreams had grown menacing. Joey seemed pale and sick. He looked malnourished and starved. With each vision, I tried to check him for bruises and scratches, for any hint of abuse, but I could never get close enough to touch him. At first, he would blankly stare at me and not say anything. Those dreams were the worst. As a few weeks passed, he moved more, even spoke. His words were few and far between, almost as if he had forgotten how to talk.

"Lost key," he would say in his scared yet gentle tone. I had no idea what he meant.

I yelled at him and begged him to tell me more. By this time, I had no doubt that he was dead, but I had to know what happened to him, at least before we moved away. Time was limited, and I only had a few days left.

"Lost key!" He screamed at me over and over, his anger growing.

"Key to what?!" I cried. It all felt real. "Tell me now, or I will never see you again! Do you hear me? We are moving away! If you are somewhere close by, tell me!"

He shivered and sobbed. "Cold. Water. Lost key."

I shook my head. "Water? The river? In the woods?" It didn't make sense.

"WATER! Lost key!" he shouted over and over again. "Cold, dark, under."

"Under?" It was a new word. Was he under something? "Where, Joey? Where?"

His body began to fade. "Home."

And within a millisecond, he was gone. I cried out to him all night in my sleep, remaining in a black room with water up to my knees. Where was he? How could he have gotten there? I stared at the darkness surrounding me, standing in what seemed like a black box. Reaching out, I tried to feel for the walls. I didn't see them at first as I ran my shin into the stairs. I tripped to the right, falling over the side of the stairway into the deeper water. I hit something as I dropped, and it fell on me, trapping me underneath the murky pool. I couldn't breathe or lift the heavy shelving that had landed on me. I screamed underwater, panicked, trying to slip through. A sharp piece of metal had cut into my leg. My torn jeans were snagged on the pointed end, pinning me further.

I jolted upright in bed and gasped for air, coughing. "Joey!" I screamed.

I knew where he was. There was no doubt about it now. I rushed out in the middle of the night with my cell phone, using the screen's light to search the backyard. "Joey!" I repeatedly screamed, nearly expecting a reply. It was cold and rainy like the night he disappeared. The wind rushed toward me, and I could have sworn I heard a faraway call. I turned, aiming my phone's flashlight at the old tornado shelter. It was impossible. Joey couldn't have been inside. It remained locked for years, and we never had the key.

"Lost key…" I rushed to the shelter, tugging on the door. "Joey! Open the door!"

I cried for him, begging him to let me in, to lead me to something that would release him. As I pulled on the door, my feet slipped in the mud. The rain fell in a torrential downpour, turning the backyard into a soupy mess. I dropped onto my face—soaked and filthy—eyed the door and sighed. I would need something out of the shed to break through the metal door. Slowly, I climbed to my feet, trying to maintain balance while I searched for my lost phone. Thanks to the flashlight, I found it rather quickly, and something shimmered in its light within the churned-up mud, something metallic. I slipped my finger through the loop of the object and gave it a sharp tug. For a long moment, I stared at the item in disbelief. It was a key—an old, rusty key.

Frantic, I shoved the key into the lock and gave it a sharp turn. It unlocked with minimal effort. I pulled the door open, and the smell immediately hit me, and I gagged. I pulled my shirt over my nose and flashed the light inside the underground shelter. The small square room had filled up halfway already. I eyed the stairway, noticing that it had mostly rotted to pieces. One step had previously snapped in half. I looked to the side, catching a wall covered in shelving. However, one section nearest the steps remained empty. I narrowed my gaze and noticed a slight sparkle underneath the water. Down there, the other wrack of shelves lay on the floor beneath the pool.

I carefully descended the slick staircase. The water rose higher by the minute. Soon, the entire place would overflow. I jumped into the water and yelped at how cold it was. The murky liquid came up to my waist as I waded to the side, trying to feel the shelf with my foot. As I ran into the solid surface, I reached into the water. I cringed when I realized I would have to dive under, but I was never good at swimming and couldn't open my eyes underwater. I flashed my phone above the splashing waves but only got a bright reflection blocking my sight.

"Sorry, phone." I quickly submerged my cell. The light illuminated the water, and there, at the bottom, lay the most terrifying thing I had ever seen. I screamed and backed away.

I wanted to retrieve my parents and make them dig through the mess. But guilt overtook me, and I turned and dove into the black water. I searched with my hands, feeling a softer material underneath the metal shelving. I tugged, but that didn't work. Instead, I lifted the shelf and rose, holding it at an angle with both arms over my head. Then, the rotting corpse of what I could only assume was my little brother floated to the top. He was bloated, disfigured, and had rotted in his fleshier areas. As tall as a seven-year-old boy, the size was correct, and the smell was atrocious. I screamed and tried to move out of the way but dropped the shelf onto myself. I fell back as the shelving plummeted atop my brother and me. My head struck the stairs behind me, and my vision blurred with a flash of white. I swallowed a mouthful of the putrid water and immediately vomited. It was nearly pitch black in the small room as my phone died and lay somewhere within the room.

"Dad!" I screamed. "Mom!"

I managed to escape the trap and scrambled up the stairs. As I reached the door, a gust of wind slammed it closed. I crashed into its surface, pounding with all my might. The door had locked behind me, and then it dawned on me. This had to have been what happened to my brother. He had lost the key and couldn't unlock the door and escape.

"He fell. He fell, hit the shelf, and was trapped. He-he drowned!" I sobbed at the idea. He couldn't even cry for help. How scared he must have been.

I reached into my pajama pocket and retrieved the key. I had to get to my parents. Cold overtook me, and I began to shiver. I felt a sharp pain in the back of my head, and I became dizzy. Lightly, I touched the back of my head. From a small gap in the door, I could barely make out a dark stain on my fingertips—blood. I had to get out of there. I lifted the key, pawing at the door to find the keyhole. I fought with the item and tried to make it fit into the slot when the stairs snapped and broke underneath my weight. I dropped into the water, losing the key in the process.

"Help," I tried to yell. I stared upward at the thin crack by the door, barely a shimmer in the blackness around me. "Dad. Mom."

I lost consciousness not long after. And still, to this day, I lay inside the black pool of water. I don't know if they ever found my or Joey's body. It gets boring here, in the darkness. I at least have Joey with me, and we will continue playing hide-and-seek, but this time with our parents in their dreams.

ABOUT THE AUTHOR

A. R. Redington is a number one Audible and Amazon best-selling author. Born and raised in Kansas, she thrived creatively at an early age, focusing on art and storytelling. Her passion for gaming and character design led her to pursue an artistic career. She attended the Rocky Mountain College of Art + Design, receiving a BFA in illustration/children's book specialization. With experience in graphic design, formatting, illustration, editing, publishing, and writing, Redington creates and designs everything for her novels while working freelance on the side.

She is the author and illustrator of the sci-fi/fantasy series The Esoteric Design, Masters of the Ellem (fantasy), Trouble with Mystery (romantic thriller), Whispers from Beyond: 30 Miniature Tales (horror), and "The Trophy" from Predator: Eyes of the Demon. You can learn more about Redington at her website: www.ARRedington.com.

9 781958 038048